Chive Right In
Isabella Proctor Cozy Mysteries
Book 7

Lisa Bouchard

LISA BOUCHARD

CHIVE RIGHT IN

This is a work of fiction. Names, characters, places, and incidents either are the product of the author's imagination or are used fictitiously, and any resemblance to actual persons, living or dead, business establishments, events, or locales is entirely coincidental.

For Paul, who supports all my dreams.

Chapter 1

You look just fine, for a human," Jameson said. I swear he was the only cat who could make a compliment sound like a dig.

I turned to my mirror. "Just fine for a human?" I frowned. I thought I looked great, and I was ready for Palmer's eyes to bug out when he saw me. I'd dressed up for Christmas dinner at his house, but tonight was an entirely different story.

Tonight, we were attending the slightly delayed Portsmouth Police Department annual New Year's Eve party. No police department threw parties on actual holidays, because they were needed on the streets. I didn't suppose much happened on January 7, though.

"Black suits you, but don't you want more flair? More color?" Jameson asked. "You could cast up a quick glamour and really dazzle them."

I turned to him. "What are you saying? I'm not dazzling enough as I am?" I'd worked hard on my hair and makeup this afternoon. It took an astonishing amount of time and product to make my hair curl perfectly and, as for the cat eye eyeliner—fifth time's the charm. Or at least fifth time was enough practice to evenly line both eyes. Yeah, some magical assistance might have come in handy. "Too late now. I'm done."

"Next time, consider it. You could have saved yourself time and money."

I walked into the living room to retrieve my new evening purse. He had a good point there. Saving time and money were part of the fundamental nature of the Proctor family. "What happens if I drink too much champagne and let the glamour slip? How would I explain that to a room full of police?"

He rolled his eyes like a teenager. "The young are rather silly. You don't let the champagne affect you. Didn't your mother teach you that spell?"

I shook my head and my curls bounced around my face. "I don't drink much. But if my cat continues to mock my fashion sense, that may change."

He stretched and walked into his room, pushing the door shut.

I paced in the living room, now doubting how I looked. Thea and Delia were giving their last "Christmas in Portsmouth" tour tonight, so neither of them were available to help me get ready. Inspiration struck, and I took a picture of myself in a full-length mirror and sent it to Hannah McGinty.

Tell me I look okay for the party

Three dots came up on my screen and I waited for her response. She sent me the wide eyes emoji, so I guess I looked fine.

The knock at my door had me put my phone in my bag. I saw Palmer through the peephole and grinned. "Who is it?" I asked.

CHIVE RIGHT IN

"Ma'am. This is the police. I need to inspect your apartment," he said with a smile.

I opened the door and leaned against the frame. "You got a warrant, buster?"

His jaw dropped and he said nothing.

Bruce's door squeaked as it opened, and I quickly pulled Palmer into my apartment. I didn't need my nosy neighbor eavesdropping on us.

"You look . . . amazing," he said.

I beamed. "Thank you. My harshest critic says I look okay, for my species."

Palmer furrowed his brow. "Who?"

"Jameson." I gestured to the roses in Palmer's hand, white with red edges. "Are those for me?"

He blushed. "Yes. I forgot about them for a minute."

I took them from him. "You'll need to stop staring at me at some point tonight. If only to drive us to the party." I had already filled a vase with water, hoping he'd bring me flowers. I set them in the water and placed the vase on the dining room table.

Now that our hands were empty, he pulled me to him. "Only for matters of safety. You're too gorgeous to look away from."

I put my arms around his neck and pulled his head down for a kiss. When we separated, I thought Jameson's idea of a glamour might have some merit. At least then I wouldn't worry about Palmer having my lipstick on his lips. "Ready to go?"

I took his outstretched arm and yelled goodnight to Jameson.

Over the course of the nine months I'd known Palmer, I'd had the chance to meet a lot of his coworkers, mostly all in the line of duty. I wasn't sure how going to a party with them would be fun. "What was last year's party like?"

Palmer turned out of my parking lot. "I didn't go. I heard it was fun, though."

"Why didn't you go?"

"We can't all go and leave the department unstaffed. I didn't have a date, and I didn't care if I went or not."

Was it wrong to be happy he hadn't had a girlfriend last year? Probably.

"People who worked last year got first choice to go to the party this year. I said yes." We stopped at a red light and he looked at me. "I wanted the entire department to see the gorgeous woman I'm dating."

I blushed. "That's very flattering. And I want the women you work with to see you're off-limits."

He chuckled. "They already do. Kate's made sure of it."

We pulled up to the valet parking stand at the Marriott on the river.

The valet opened my door. I got out and waited for Palmer to join me on the sidewalk. Kate stepped out of the car behind us. "Woah," I whispered. Kate's floor-length red dress with plunging neckline and swirling patterns of crystal embellishments made her look like she was ready for the Oscars. "Oh my gosh, you're stunning."

She beamed at me. "Thanks. Don't tell anyone, but this was the dress I wore to my senior prom."

Palmer joined me. "Kate, you look lovely."

"Thanks, boss. You look . . . about the same." She touched the arm of the man standing next to her. "This is my friend, Mikey Dunn."

Palmer stretched his hand out. "Steve Palmer. Nice to meet you, Mikey."

Mikey shook Palmer's hand, but looked like he wasn't sure it was his best course of action.

"Let's head inside," I said while trying not to shiver. My wrap was perfect for a warm car, but it didn't block the icy wind coming off the Piscataqua River.

I'd never been to a party like this, and I wasn't sure what to expect. I'd never even gone to a prom in school. Thea, Delia, and I had considered going to the junior prom without dates but, as the resident "weird girls," we were pretty sure no one would ask us to dance, and we'd wind up sitting together in a corner. Why do that when we could be home, not wearing high heels, having actual fun?

Palmer took our seating card and walked us to our table. Kate grabbed hers and followed us. "We're at the same table, good," she said.

"Can I get you ladies a drink?" Palmer asked.

"Seltzer with lime, please," I said.

Kate asked for the same.

Palmer stared at Mikey, who made no move to get his date a drink. "Mikey," Palmer prompted.

It took Mikey a beat to realize what Palmer wanted. "Oh, right. I'll be back in a minute."

As I watched them walk off to the bar, I said, "Where did you find him?"

Kate sighed. "He's a friend from school. You wouldn't believe how hard it is to find a date when you're a cop."

"Really?"

"Once you discount all the ones who can't resist asking about your handcuffs, yes."

I laughed. "Not exactly the thing you ask about before your first date, that's for sure."

"And I didn't want to ask anyone I work with, so my choices weren't . . . great."

"Probably not best to date coworkers. Tell me, when is your birthday? I want to take you out for a drink."

"Not until July."

"It's a date, then."

"But speaking of birthdays," Kate said conspiratorially, "Palmer's is next Saturday."

"Good to know. I'll have to plan a surprise."

Palmer and Mikey returned with our drinks. I smiled up at Palmer. "Thank you."

He sat next to me and took my hand in his. "Dinner is in an hour, but there are hors d'oeuvres if you're hungry."

I took a sip of my water. "In a few minutes." I turned to Mikey. "Have you and Kate been friends for long?"

He looked up from his bottle of beer. "We did drama together in high school. I was a senior when she was a freshman, so I didn't know her all that well. I ran into her at the grocery store a few months ago, and we got to talking. I graduated from college in June and moved home with my parents."

"Interesting. What did you study?" I asked.

"A little of this, a little of that. I wanted to be an engineer, but wound up with a criminal justice degree."

"Do you work for the department?" I asked.

He looked at the table, then back at me. "I hope to. I'd like to move out of my parents' house. Can you believe my mother turned my room into a hot yoga studio, and now I have to live in the basement?"

Music started and Palmer leaned in close. "Let's dance."

"Absolutely," I said.

When he brought me out to the dance floor, he said, "Mikey will never work for the department. I ran his name as part of his application and . . . let's just say there were several lapses of judgment while he was a student."

I looked up into Palmer's deep brown eyes. I didn't want to talk about Mikey, but I had one question. "Does Kate know?"

"I didn't know they were friends. I'll tell her on Monday."

He pulled me in closer, and I forgot all about Kate, Mikey, and the rest of the party as we danced. We didn't stop until the music did. Palmer led me back to our table, where the chief, Papatonis, and his date had joined us.

"This is my fiancée, Lourdes," Papatonis said once we sat. "Lourdes, this is Detective Steve Palmer and his girlfriend, Isabella Proctor."

"Nice to meet you, Lourdes," I said.

She smiled and nodded, but didn't say anything. She bit her lip and looked to Papatonis. The poor woman was clearly intimidated.

"I'd like to freshen up before dinner. Kate, Lourdes, would you join me?"

I was grateful that Kate and Lourdes stood up. It was silly to need to use the bathroom in groups, but I thought if Kate and I could talk to Lourdes for a minute, she might relax a little and have fun.

Once we were in the hallway, I stopped. "Lourdes, are you okay?"

She nodded.

"Because you don't look it. Can we do anything to help?"

Lourdes stopped biting her lip and looked from me to Kate. "I'm at a table with Luke's boss and his chief. I'm terrified I'm going to do something to hurt his career."

After what Palmer had told me about Mikey, there was no way she could be the worst date at the table.

"You'll be fine once you relax. My date's been arrested in the past. I'm sure you can't top that," Kate said.

I said nothing, thinking Palmer could fill Kate in on Monday and that I didn't want to ruin her night. "He has?"

Kate nodded. "He doesn't know that I know but, after tonight, I'm not seeing him again."

"Lourdes, I think you're going to be fine. Papa—Luke obviously loves you. Kate and I like you already, and I've got a lot of sway with Palmer and the chief," I said.

Lourdes frowned. "You know the chief?"

"Since I was a baby. We're all friends at our table, so try to relax and have fun."

She blew out a deep breath. "I'll try."

We walked back into the party and I almost ran into Max Hathaway, the night coroner, as he was leaving. "Hi Max, nice to see you here."

He looked down at me. "Oh, hi. Can I talk to you outside?"

"Lead the way."

Once we were halfway across the hotel lobby, he stopped walking. "That guy with Detective Palmer, is he really Kate's date?"

I grimaced. "He is. But she was desperate for a date and asked him as a last resort. She's already said she's not interested in him."

Max's shoulders sagged. "He was her last resort?"

I realized I should have phrased that better. "Oh, Max, that's not what I meant. I know you like her, but I'm not sure she knows. Maybe ask her out for coffee someday, you know, try to spend some time with her outside of work."

"That's what I was going to do tonight, but then she shows up with him."

I put my hand on his arm. "Do you want to join our table? I'm sure we can squeeze you in."

He shook his head. "No. I don't want to look like the loser who couldn't get a date. I'm just going home."

"Promise me you'll call her tomorrow and ask her for coffee?"

He didn't promise, but he didn't say he wouldn't, either, as he walked away.

Chapter 2

I took a sip of my white chocolate mocha and leaned back in my office chair, proud of myself for finally getting the hang of running my business. I'd managed to order in advance all the potion-making ingredients I thought I'd need for the next three months. No rushing around to find what I needed, no paying for overnight shipping. Now all I had to do was spend a solid week in the prep room creating potions, salves, and tinctures from the inventory I currently had.

I pulled up my notes app and walked out to the shop floor to do a quick inventory. Mackenzie was chatting with Mrs. Rothman, whose sciatica was acting up again. "I can absolutely sell you the muscle relaxant salve, but if you don't go out for a walk every day, I'll be selling it to you forever."

Mrs. Rothman smiled. "That's easy for you to say, you're young. It takes serious effort to get out for a walk at my age."

Mackenzie looked skeptical. "You're forty-five. You're not old. Trust me, if you walk a half an hour every day this week, you'll be amazed at how much better you feel."

Mrs. Rothman took the jar of salve. "You know the weather is terrible, right?"

"You know an inexpensive gym is ten dollars a month, right?"

Ooh! Game, set, and match to my assistant. "Fine. I'll do it, but only so I can prove you wrong," Mrs. Rothman conceded.

I got back to my inventory, pleased with how well Mackenzie fit into the shop and its vibe. Our customers didn't come here for just tea or remedies, they came in to take charge of their own well-being. Sometimes they just needed a little help to do the right thing. She instinctively knew how to talk to the customers to get them to do the right thing. "Nice work with Mrs. Rothman," I said once she'd left.

Mackenzie rolled her eyes and smiled. "I've been telling her the same thing every week for a good month now. It's about time she listened to me."

"Only a month, that's good. I'm going to be working in the prep room for the rest of the day, so come find me if you need anything," I told her, not thinking she'd actually need anything. I was amazed at how confident I felt leaving the store in her hands.

"No problem, boss," she said.

Once in the prep room, I started pulling down ingredients for a new potion I'd created that boosted a person's immune reaction. Before I could start the potion, I heard Hope's voice in my mind.

Good afternoon, ladies. It's time to get back to work. We'll meet tonight at seven, at Proctor House.

This was not what I needed to finish out my day. We hadn't met since the disastrous night the sorority abandoned me to watch over a neighborhood on my own and, honestly, I hadn't gotten over it yet. I had asked for their help safeguarding a neighborhood that had seen two murders in the space of a few days and, while they hadn't said no, they came out with the most perfunctory effort and then went home, leaving me on my own.

I didn't know how to deal with people who disliked like me for any good reason. I didn't think being young was a good reason to not like me. Being young and having a familiar, though, was a good enough reason for them. I'd spoken to my grandmother, and she wasn't a lot of help. She was more inclined to ignore people who didn't like her and not worry about it. I'd rather work with people than around them. Grandma said I'll grow out of that by the time I hit fifty.

I really hoped she was wrong, because working with other witches made me happy.

Once I closed the shop at six, I went straight to Proctor House. If I was going to work with my sorority tonight, I was going to need a good dinner and some time with people who loved me first. Aunt Nadia was pulling a lasagna out of the oven when I walked into the kitchen. "Smells fantastic," I said.

She set the pan on a trivet. "You're here early. Give it five minutes to cool down and then help yourself. I've got to help your grandmother with a spell. And pull the rolls out of the oven when the timer rings."

I raised an eyebrow at my aunt. "What kind of spell?"

She hung her apron on a peg by the stove. "No clue. She didn't tell me anything other than it had to be done before we ate."

What was Grandma getting up to now? I shook my head and grabbed a plate. We'd all find out soon enough.

16

CHIVE RIGHT IN

Thea and Delia were laughing as they came in from the driveway. "And then, when he fell for the third time, I thought his pants were going to split!" Thea said.

"I don't know why people don't trust you when you tell them they won't be able to stand on the slipperiest ice Mother Nature ever made," Delia said.

Thea rolled her eyes. "Some people can't resist taking the challenge, and we can't resist laughing at them when they do."

I dished out three plates of lasagna, then pulled the rolls out of the oven. Rolls used to be my job, but I'd become too busy since I'd inherited the Portsmouth Apothecary to think about what I used to do at Proctor House. Before I could think about the sadness that came with that thought, Delia started asking me questions.

"Sorority meeting tonight?"

I sat at the table and took the fork and napkin Thea handed me. "Yes. We haven't met since before Christmas."

"Think they'll start acting better?" Thea asked.

I took a bite of lasagna and shook my head. They had no reason to start liking me more now, and I doubted time away from each other would fix the underlying issues. Not for the first time, I wondered why Mrs. Thompson thought I'd be a good fit in this group of witches.

Delia put the rolls and garlic butter on the table. "I'm sure Hope will figure something out."

"I hope so. I'm not sure what I'll do if she doesn't. No one wants to be part of a group that doesn't like you, but I don't want to give up Jameson or the amulet. So I guess I'll stay and just wear them down with persistence."

Aunt Lily and my mother walked into the kitchen. "Good evening, girls," Aunt Lily said.

They served themselves dinner and joined us. We ate dinner and chatted about inconsequential things—the perfect relaxation I needed before my meeting.

At five minutes before seven, the rest of my sorority and three other women I'd never met came to the kitchen door. My mother let them in and offered them dinner. "Thank you, Michelle, but we've already eaten," Hope said. "Isabella, come with us. We have a lot to do tonight and need to start right away."

I looked at the last few bites of my dinner and sighed. Before I looked up at Hope, I pasted a smile on my face. "I'm ready to go."

"Your grandmother said we should use the formal dining room tonight," Hope told me.

I stood up. "Follow me."

Once we all sat at the large table in the red dining room, Hope started the meeting. "I'd like to introduce you to three witches from the California sorority. Their leader, Inanna Blackwing, is here to observe our group dynamics and adjust them so that we work well together."

An older woman with black, frizzy hair and a wart on the tip of her nose smiled. "Yes. Hope tells me there's a problem accepting the newest member into the sorority. These kinds of problems are common enough, particularly when a younger witch joins an established group, and I'm sure we can work through the issue with a minimum of fuss."

That wasn't exactly the problem. Helen was the newest member but, because she was older, the other members didn't have any issue with her. Should I correct Inanna? I decided to let Hope deal with the misunderstanding.

"Inanna has brought two other members of her sorority with her, Raven Stone and Winter Hart. They'll be working with you in smaller groups for the week."

A short woman with curly gray hair and laugh lines around her eyes smiled. "I'm Raven."

The third woman, Winter, looked nothing like her name. Her warm, ochre skin and gold-streaked hair made her look like the embodiment of summer. "I'm Winter. We're all happy to be here to show how our coven of fifty-three witches gets along and works like a team."

"The problem as I see it," Anna said, "is that one of us acts like she's better than the rest of us. We each had to earn our familiars and hers was given to her, even before she joined the sorority. She's also hoarding two other familiars, most likely to give them to her cousins rather than those of our members here who have gone without for too long."

Inanna looked at Hope, who gave her an I-told-you-so look.

"And you are?" Inanna asked.

"Anna."

Inanna leaned forward. "Tell me, Anna, how you think that was a helpful comment."

I marveled at how Inanna managed to sound like she was correcting a kindergartener while still conveying that Anna had made a terrible mistake.

Anna smirked. "I wasn't sure Hope would give you the whole story. She's been friends with Isabella's grandmother since they were young, and it's no secret to any of us that has bought Isabella a place in the sorority, and her familiar."

Sasha leaned back and shook her head. While it wasn't support, at least I knew not everyone felt like Anna. It didn't even matter that Anna wasn't telling the whole truth. It was Mrs. Thompson who gave me Jameson and the amulet, not Hope. From what I could see, Hope had no choice but to allow me into the sorority.

"It seems that not everyone agrees with your assessment."

Anna opened her mouth to speak, but made no sound.

"I'd like you to think about how your words affect others before you speak again," Inanna said. "Maybe an hour will do."

Anna tried to speak again, her face turning red as she attempted to yell. As much as I liked the idea of Anna not being able to lie, the thought that Inanna was willing to cast a spell on her to keep her from speaking was frightening. She'd barely met us, didn't even know our names, and already she was casting what could be considered a harmful spell on one of us.

"No one likes it when a woman succeeds because of her family connections. Or when she takes what never really belonged to her. Unfortunately, we have to deal with these people whether we want to or not."

Was she talking about me? I'd never taken something that didn't belong to me, but I was sure my entire sorority thought I only got Jameson because I came from a prominent family. I looked to Hope, who shook her head. I stayed quiet and waited to see what else was in store for us tonight.

"We're going to break into two groups. Raven will take Anna, Sasha, and Christina. Winter will take Claire, Isabella, and Helen.

CHIVE RIGHT IN

We filed out to the backyard. This didn't bode well for us. It was cold outside, but I wasn't going to be the first to complain, or the first to use a spell to keep myself warm.

Inanna stood in front of us. "I want each group to stand on opposite sides of the yard. You'll start with the same group exercise, and once you've mastered it, the two groups will challenge each other."

My group turned to follow Winter to the rose bushes by the back fence.

"Isabella, I'd like to speak to you for a moment," Inanna said.

My group walked off without me, and I stood, alone, with the most frightening witch I'd ever met.

"You may think your problems are over now that I'm here to sort out the mess you've made with your sorority. They're not. I'm going to do whatever it takes to convince Hope that you're too young to be here. She can invite you back in thirty years, if you're lucky."

"But what about Mrs. Thompson? She was the witch who said I belong here."

Inanna scoffed. "Beatrice Thompson was a sentimental old fool. She was one of the weakest sorority members I'd ever seen, aside from you, and no one took her seriously."

I said nothing as I felt my confidence crumble. I'd held on to the idea that I was special because Mrs. T. chose me. Inanna ripped that away from me in less than a minute.

"Go join your group, and don't discuss this with anyone."

I walked away, tears of humiliation threatening to spill out of my eyes.

When I joined my group, Winter said, "Now that we're all here, let's start with a basic training exercise." A glowing ball of light appeared over her outstretched hand.

I pulled up the shield around the backyard, hoping none of the neighbors saw the light appear from nowhere.

"Not this again," Claire complained. She made a face and rubbed her neck. "It's the wrong season for bees, isn't it?"

Winter stepped forward, closer to Claire. "I understand Hope tried this exercise with you and there were problems. Inanna decided you needed to try again, only this time there are consequences for not working together. Nothing bad, just a little zap, like a dog feels when it gets too close to an electric fence. But each time you disobey me, talk back, or do anything else I see as not working together as a team, the zap will get stronger."

She stepped back and looked at the three of us. "I don't want to hurt you. That's all in your control though."

I didn't appreciate being trained like a dog, but I wasn't going to complain and get zapped. I didn't see the point of forcing us to work together, either. It was obvious the California witches had been brought in because no one wanted to work with me. Hurting our New Hampshire members until they gave in didn't seem like it would be effective once they left.

Winter passed the light to Claire. "You know how this works, ladies. Gently toss the orb to each other."

Claire tossed the orb to Helen, who tossed it to Winter. "I'm not part of your training group," Winter said as she tossed it back to Claire.

Claire threw it to me, faster than she had to Winter, but I caught it. I tossed it to Helen. "You call that a pass? It barely got here."

Winter frowned at Helen, and Helen yelped and rubbed her neck. "That hurts!"

Winter grinned maliciously. "Oh, I'm sorry. Did I forget to tell you that the spell gets a little worse each time I use it?"

This was not okay. I looked over to Hope, but she had her back to me. *Hey, Hope. You know they're hurting us when we don't behave, right?*

Hope's shoulders stiffened, but she didn't turn or respond in any way.

"Hey! Cut that out!" I heard from across the lawn. Sasha must have gotten a strong zap.

I almost missed the light, but caught it with a wobble. I needed to pay attention to the exercise and try to keep from being zapped. I tossed the light to Claire. What was the other group doing that they would get zapped? They'd been working together for years—decades even—why did Sasha get zapped?

I felt a zap on my neck. It stung, but not even as badly as a mosquito bite. "Pay attention, Isabella," Winter warned.

That didn't hurt so bad. Either Claire and Helen had a low pain threshold, or Winter had lied about it always getting worse.

Inanna clapped her hands and the lights extinguished. "All right, ladies, it's time for our second exercise. Everyone come together in a circle."

We did as she said, and I hoped the zapping portion of the evening was over.

"You don't seem ready to challenge each other yet. As sorority witches, you need to be prepared for pain. I'll be working with Hope to toughen you New Hampshire witches up."

Toughen us up? That didn't sound like a good idea and it could cause some of the other members to leave.

"What did we learn from the exercise?" Inanna asked.

No one wanted to say anything, probably because they didn't want to get it wrong.

"There will be no penalties for telling the truth," Hope said.

"I learned that Isabella gets preferential treatment because she's a Proctor, and there's nothing we can do about that," Claire said.

Preferential treatment? I sighed. "Look, I didn't ask for any of this. I didn't even know Mrs. Thompson was a witch for most of the time she was my neighbor. I had no idea about the sorority and certainly never asked to be part of it. I was pulled in, against the better judgment of my entire family, and told it was too late because I had the amulet and the familiar."

I took a deep breath. "And now I'm stuck in a group where I'm resented for what other people have forced on me. I'm trying to contribute to the group, follow the rules, and use my power to keep us safe."

Before I continued, I looked at each witch in the circle. "I don't know what else I can do to earn your respect. I don't think this was a good idea—forcing you to play nice or feel pain—but I had nothing to do with that. So here I am, in a group of people that hate me, won't work with me and, yet, I'm duty bound to stay."

Inanna put her hand up and I stopped talking. "Think back to when you joined the sorority. How did the other witches treat you? Were you made to feel welcome? Did anyone tell you that you didn't belong and you should give up your amulet and familiar?"

Everyone else shook their heads.

"Exactly," Inanna continued. "How would you have felt? What would you have done?"

"I'd have quit," Christina said.

"Right. But she hasn't. You may not like her, you may resent her because she's young and has things it took you much longer to get, but you can at least respect her for staying. Training is over for the night. Go home and reflect on tonight's lesson."

I blinked back tears. I never considered that being my stubborn self was worthy of respect.

Several witches teleported away, but Christina remained behind. "I never considered that this could be tough on you."

I didn't have time to reply, because she teleported away.

"All right, ladies, let's get back inside," Hope said. "We've got a lot to think about tonight."

Chapter 3

We followed Inanna and Hope back into Proctor House. What had just happened? Was this whole exercise just to push me over the edge and tell people how I felt? Broomsticks, if I'd known that would have worked, I'd have done it weeks ago.

"Why don't we head into the kitchen, and I can make tea for everyone?" I asked. I didn't care so much about tea, but the unfilled cream puffs that were cooling on the counter had my attention. A little ice cream, chocolate sauce, and we'd all feel better about our night.

Grandma was taking ice cream out of the freezer when we walked in. "Nadia told me to put out the cream puffs when you got back."

"We're not here to eat and have social time, Esther," Inanna said. "Your life may have been all roses and bouncing babies, but many of us have to focus on keeping the world safe."

I gave Grandma a kiss on the cheek. I knew she was there to keep an eye on the witches and make sure I was being treated well. "Thanks, Grandma."

I set the table while everyone else sat. No one spoke, and the awkward silence stretched on until Grandma finally broke it. "I see everyone else from the New Hampshire sorority has left. Does that mean they've learned their lesson, or did they run off again, refusing to work with Isabella?"

"Esther, I told you I needed to take care of this without your help," Hope said.

Grandma ladled the warm chocolate sauce into a bowl and set it on the table. "Not trying to help, just want a status update."

My back was turned to the table when I heard a loud thud. I turned around to see Jameson, wreathed in smoke, splayed out with one paw in the chocolate sauce. The smoke vanished, but the smell of singed fur remained. "What happened? Are you hurt?"

He pulled his paw out of the chocolate. He shook his head. *Just a little. I'll be okay.*

"Is that blood under your nails? Where have you been?" I asked.

The rest of the witches in the room looked concerned. "What can we do?" Inanna asked.

I wet a paper towel and began to clean Jameson's paws, dessert forgotten. His pulse seemed normal, and I couldn't feel anything else wrong with him. "Have you been picking fights with other cats?"

He licked his now-clean paw, then rubbed his face. "No. I was trying to save my sister, but I'm not strong enough on my own."

Batwings! "But we said we'd help. Why did you go alone?"

He looked up at me, with all the disappointment his face could hold. *I can't wait for you all to decide to get along. My sister needs me. I've tried everything I can think of.* He lay his head down on the table. "I've tried, and I can't do it alone."

I petted him, feeling for more injuries. How difficult it must have been for my arrogant, snarky familiar to admit he couldn't do something. I buried my nose in his fur. "I'm sorry I let you down."

Inanna stood and paced the room. "You mean to tell me you've got a familiar being held hostage?" She glared at Hope. "And you didn't tell me? How can I get this sorority back on track when I don't even know the problems you're dealing with?"

Hope flushed. "I can handle my own sorority. I asked for help with one issue and, once that's resolved, we'll be able to handle the rest of the challenges we face."

Inanna sniffed. "That doesn't seem likely." She sat back down and addressed Jameson. "The California sorority can help. I assume the fraternity has your sister?"

Jameson nodded. He was exhausted and had already spoken to the other witches twice. I would have to relay answers to the rest of the witches in the room.

"What's preventing her from teleporting herself away?" Inanna asked.

She's under the tightest containment spell I've ever seen. I haven't even been able to weaken it.

"Where is she being held?" Winter asked.

Chandler House, in Manchester.

Chandler House? I'd been there on school trips to learn about New Hampshire history. I had no idea it was a fraternity-owned building. "It's a huge building—thirty rooms. Chandler House in Manchester."

Raven frowned. "Does every house in New Hampshire have a name? I didn't think New Hampshire was so pretentious, what with all the plaid flannel around."

I smiled. They'd come at peak flannel season, when it was common to see men dressed in two different plaids as though they looked good. "No, only the old houses. I don't know why the fraternity wanted Chandler House, it doesn't have any connection to witches that I know of."

Winter leaned forward in her chair to help herself to a cream puff. "I get that rescuing her is the right thing to do, but what's in it for us?"

I took the chocolate off the table—even if Jameson's other paw hadn't had blood on it, I needed to make a fresh batch. I couldn't barter away Jameson's family in exchange for their assistance, so I didn't say anything. I didn't have to; Inanna said what I was thinking.

"Winter," she said in a low voice, "Not everything has to be of immediate benefit to you. Try thinking about the greater good once in a while. Or at least how much better it is if we deprive the fraternity of new familiars."

"What I don't understand is why you haven't taken care of this already," Raven said. "Oh, wait, never mind. Your sorority isn't going to help you."

I poured cream into a saucepan, added semi-sweet chocolate, and started to stir them over the warm stovetop. "I hope that someday they'll come around."

"They will. They need to get to know you better. They need to look past your age and see what you bring to the sorority and then they'll forget these made-up reasons they think they don't like you," Hope said.

I took the chocolate sauce off the stove and poured it into a bowl. "Are you sure?"

"I wouldn't be so sure," Inanna interrupted. "Hope, your sorority is a mess. Why you ever let Isabella's predecessor choose her own replacement is beyond me."

"I don't let my people do anything. They do what they think is best, and we work to support each other."

Inanna rolled her eyes. "There's your problem. You're not really their leader. When I tell my witches what to do, they do it. No hesitation, no questions. I have to be that way, because I've got too many witches to manage."

I put the bowl on the table, sat, and resumed petting Jameson. I'd never seen two witches fight before about magic. Sure, my family has argued about things but, when it came to magic, we listened to each other and then usually just did whatever Grandma said. It hadn't steered us wrong yet.

"I only have six, and maybe four are a problem. Christina seems to be coming around, and I'm sure the others will follow. And I don't have to use pain or force my witches to get them to work together," Hope said.

Inanna barked a short laugh. "That's just it, Hope, they aren't working together. You'd gotten nowhere until I started with the tiniest of incentives today. Now, you've got one witch out of the four changing her tune. Give me another day, and I'll have them all in line."

Dread curled in the pit of my stomach. Sasha's yell didn't make it sound like Inanna was using the tiniest of incentives.

Hope banged the table with her hand. "No. I'm not going to let you hurt them more tomorrow. You'll have to come up with something else."

CHIVE RIGHT IN

My Aunt Lily pushed open the kitchen door, Aunt Nadia and my mother right behind her. "What's going on in here? We can hear you yelling all over the house."

Aunt Nadia focused on Jameson, who was asleep on the table. "Jameson!"

He lifted his head and looked at her. I was amazed the banging on the table didn't disturb him, but Aunt Nadia calling his name woke him right up.

Aunt Nadia scooped him up. "What happened? Never mind, don't tell me. We'll get you fixed up in no time." She took him out to the living room and, when the door closed behind her, I couldn't hear what she was doing.

"Maybe we should take a break, ladies," my mother suggested. "It's been a trying evening, and I'm sure everything will look better in the morning."

Inanna stood. "I hope you're right, Michelle. I'll be spending the rest of my night trying to plan a cat rescue and figuring out what to do with this failure of a coven."

LISA BOUCHARD

Chapter 4

Jameson and I stayed at Proctor House, anticipating more coven work first thing in the morning. Aunt Nadia had healed his singed fur and skin before we fell asleep in my old bedroom. I woke to Jameson's tail tickling my nose. "Cut it out," I mumbled. "I'm awake."

"About time. I'm hungry," he said.

I rolled over onto my back. "Then go eat. You are as capable as I am of feeding yourself and, if you even look at Aunt Nadia, she'll make you something delicious. You don't even have to ask."

Jameson yawned. "That's not special. She's ready with food whenever the sorority meets here, and you don't ask her to."

Aunt Nadia had always been like that, and I felt a twinge of guilt that I'd added so much to her workload and not thanked her. I threw the blankets off and pulled on my robe. "Okay, let's go. I'll make her sit and enjoy some tea while I help."

The clock in the kitchen read seven thirty. I scowled at Jameson. "You could have let me sleep in a bit."

Aunt Nadia set a plate of cold tuna at Jameson's seat. "Too much salmon isn't good for you."

I gave Aunt Nadia a hug. "Good morning."

"What was that for?" she asked.

I took the wooden spoon from her hand. "Jameson pointed out that you've been doing a lot more cooking for the sorority, and I haven't thanked you for it. You sit and I'll make you some tea."

"And finish scrambling the eggs?"

"Absolutely." I gave the eggs a quick stir and turned the kettle on. Aunt Nadia didn't need anything special in her tea, from a herbalist point of view, so I made her rose hip and lemon tea. As I poured the water into her mug, I saw the eggs stirring themselves. "That's cheating."

She took the mug from me. "I'd rather cheat than have overcooked eggs."

That was a fair point. "What else can I make while you're relaxing this morning?"

"You can cut up the cantaloupe and put it in a bowl."

Grandma came into the kitchen and sat. "Morning, Grandma. I'm cooking while Aunt Nadia has a short break."

"You're not burning anything, are you?"

I smiled. I wasn't a great cook, but I was trying to learn. Palmer had been teaching me to make easy but delicious things, like five-minute artisan bread and roasted brussels sprouts. "Not today. Aunt Nadia is still supervising."

"In that case, I'll have a cup of coffee and eggs when they're ready."

"I suppose the California witches are still on West Coast time and won't be down for another two hours," Aunt Nadia said.

I put the sliced cantaloupe into the bowl and inspected the eggs. "I suppose it all depends on how early Inanna wants to get to work today. The earlier she decides to get started, the worse it's going to be."

With one last stir to break up the large pieces, I put the eggs onto a platter and brought them to the table. "I'm sure we'll all know when she's ready to start."

Thea and Delia walked into the kitchen, talking about the tour they were planning for the summer. Thea wanted to call it Boats and Brews while Delia wanted Ships and Shots.

"I vote for Ships and Shots. Boats are small and dull, but ships are cool and historic," I said, even though they hadn't asked for my opinion. I thought I should have a say, because they asked me to create a signature iced tea for people who didn't want alcohol on their tour.

"Where's everyone else?" Delia asked.

"Not up yet. It's not even five in the morning for them," Aunt Nadia said.

My cousins grabbed a blueberry muffin each and headed out the door. "See you tonight," Thea called as the door closed.

I sat and helped myself to eggs and a muffin. "Grandma, I don't think I like what's going on with Inanna. It doesn't feel right to me."

She set her mug down. "What do you mean?"

I sighed. "I don't know what Hope told you, but Inanna was using a spell that zapped us if we didn't do what she wanted. I got zapped once and it wasn't so bad, but Sasha yelled so loud I could hear her across the yard."

"No, Hope didn't tell me. She wasn't happy with the night, especially after Jameson came home, but she didn't want to talk about it. She said she'd figure it out herself."

I frowned. "I hope she came up with something, because I'd be mad—I am mad that people got hurt."

"We can talk to Hope when she comes down, then together we'll be a united front to talk to Inanna and make her change tactics."

I was relieved. With family by my side, I felt like I could do anything.

The clock read eight thirty when Winter and Raven walked into the kitchen. "Have you seen Inanna?" Winter asked.

Aunt Nadia shook her head. "I've been up for two hours and haven't seen her. She's probably still asleep."

Raven shook her head. "I knocked on her door and, when she didn't answer, I peeked in. She wasn't there."

"Do either of you know her morning routine? Maybe she goes for a long walk before breakfast every day," Grandma suggested, frowning at the thought of so much exercise.

Winter shrugged. "Let me try her telepathically."

After a moment, she shook her head. "Nothing."

I looked to Grandma. Was that even possible? The few times I'd telepathically spoken to someone, I'd felt them before I spoke. "You mean she didn't answer you?"

Winter bit her lip. "I couldn't find her."

Grandma stood. "Let me get Hope. She may be able to find her."

I hoped that would work. Maybe Inanna had put up a psychic Do Not Disturb sign that only an older witch could break through.

"While we're waiting, help yourself to breakfast," Aunt Nadia said. I poured each of us more coffee and sat, hoping this didn't mean what I thought it might.

Five minutes later, Grandma called me into the living room. "It's time to call the police. We can't find her anywhere."

My heart sank. "You think she's dead?"

Hope nodded. "I've always been able to find people. Do you have any contacts in the morgue?"

I was about to say no, when I realized I did. Kate's friend Max. "Let me call Kate, she's got a friend."

Grandma put her hand on my arm. "Do it outside, I don't want to upset Winter and Raven until we know something."

I nodded and called Kate once I was behind the large willow tree in the backyard.

"Hey Isabella, what's up? I'm dying to get lunch and talk about the party," Kate said when she picked up her phone.

"Oh, I'd like that, too, but I'm calling in more of a professional capacity."

I heard her open the notebook she always kept with her. Her voice was serious when she said, "Okay. Tell me everything."

"We've got houseguests at Proctor House, and one of them is gone."

"It hasn't been forty-eight hours yet, has it?" she asked.

"No. I saw her last night, but she's elderly, a friend of the family, and we're worried. I thought we could see Max, and I hoped he'd let me take a peek at any Jane Does he has."

"Sure. Are you at your apartment or Proctor House? I can pick you up in ten minutes either way."

"Thanks, Kate. I'm at the house, and I'll wait for you outside."

True to her word, Kate was at the house in ten minutes. "I called Max, and he's going to meet us there. He says an older woman came in early this morning."

I closed my eyes. "Hey, it might not be her," Kate reassured me.

I was too worried about Inanna to make small talk while we drove. When we got to the hospital, I rushed ahead of Kate, needing to know who was lying in the morgue.

Max was waiting for us at the elevator. "Thanks for coming back out, Max. I appreciate it. I'll try not to take up much of your time."

He smiled at me, then looked at Kate. "It's no problem. Anything for a friend of Kate's."

He opened the door to the morgue but didn't walk in. "I know you've been here before but, if you feel woozy, I want you to sit down immediately. The floors are hard, and I don't want you to get a concussion if you faint."

I nodded, trying to ignore the roiling in my stomach. I took time for a quick plea to Brigid. *Please don't let her be here.*

We followed Max in. He pulled a drawer out of the wall that had a body covered in a blue sheet. "Are you ready?"

Kate grabbed my hand. "I'm here."

I nodded and Max pulled the sheet down so I could see Inanna's face with a scorch mark from the middle of her forehead to her right ear.

My legs started to buckle, but I got hold of myself. "The scorch mark is new," I told Kate.

Max put Inanna's body away and helped Kate bring me to his office. "Sit," he commanded.

I did as he told me. "That's Inanna."

"Like the Mesopotamian goddess?" Max asked as he poured me a finger of whiskey. "Drink this, you'll feel better."

I took the glass. I knew it would help, but Grandma always put our trauma whiskey in tea. It seemed wrong to drink it straight, especially this early in the morning. I took a sip and set the glass on his desk. "Thanks. It's a little early for me."

"What can you tell me about her?" Kate asked.

I closed my eyes. "She's a friend of Grandma's friend Hope. Her name is Inanna Blackwing, and she's from California."

"Okay, that's good. Do you know what she was doing last night? Or where she could have gone to get that burn on her face?"

I shook my head. I had a theory, but I wasn't going to tell Kate that Inanna went to rescue a talking magical cat from a museum in Manchester. I'd let Palmer and the chief figure out how much to tell her. "Maybe Grandma would know," I said.

"I'll take you home and talk to her."

Kate stood up, but I kept staring at the floor. Another witch staying at Proctor House was dead. Was the house cursed?

"Isabella," Kate said gently.

I looked up. "Oh, right. Let's go."

"I'm sorry for your loss," Kate said as she started her car.

"Thanks. It's Hope who is going to be most upset. And the two other women who were visiting with Inanna."

Kate's eyes widened. "She didn't travel alone? How well do you know the other two women?"

I closed my eyes and leaned my head on the window. "Not at all. They've only been here for a day. We spent some time together last night, but I don't know that we're ever going to be friends or anything."

"I'll have to talk to them as well."

I wondered what kind of working relationship the California sorority had with the police. I needed to warn them Kate was coming. "Do you want me to call ahead?"

"No. I need to see their reactions when they get the news." She hit speed dial on her phone.

"Palmer."

"Hey, boss. I'm in a car with Isabella."

Was it my imagination, or could I feel him tensing up over the phone?

"What's up?"

"She's tentatively identified a Jane Doe in the morgue. I'm bringing her home to talk to people there who knew the victim. Want to meet me there?"

"On my way."

He hung up without saying a word to me.

"Are you going to have anyone else ID the body?"

"Palmer will bring someone down after we've questioned them." She paused for a moment, then kept talking. "Look, Isabella, we're friends, right?"

This didn't sound good. "Yes. At least I think so."

"This is the second dead body in a year that's been linked to your family's house. If there's anything you want to tell me before we get there . . ."

"You mean like someone in my family is a murderer? We caught the guy who killed Hester, and he wasn't related to me."

We stopped at a red light and she looked at me. "I know it sounds like I'm accusing your family, but I have to ask. It's starting to look like a pattern. Not that I think you have anything to do with it, but . . ."

"No, Kate. No one in my family is a murderer. I can see why you think you need to ask, but it's not us."

Our light turned green and she started to drive. "Good."

"That's it? No cross-examination? This wasn't much of an interrogation," I teased.

Her lips curled into a grin. "Don't need more. I can usually tell when someone is lying to me, and you're not. Palmer says I need to lean into my intuition more, because it doesn't steer me wrong."

She seemed done talking to me, so I contacted Grandma quickly. Kate and Palmer will be at the house soon. Inanna was in the morgue, and they want to talk to all of us. Kate says not to tell Winter and Raven, she wants to see their first reaction.

Message received.

LISA BOUCHARD

Chapter 5

The chief was waiting for us in the driveway of Proctor House. "Hey, Chief."

He nodded to us. "Kate. Isabella. I'm sorry for your loss."

"Thank you, but I didn't really know her well." I looked around. "Is Palmer here?"

"No. I wanted to talk to your family myself."

My eyes widened. This sounded bad. Like we were all in trouble and maybe going to jail bad. We followed the chief up the driveway, and Aunt Lily opened the door for us. "Ray," she said.

"Lily. Bad news, I'm afraid."

Aunt Lily stepped aside. "Everyone's in the living room."

The living room was silent except for the crackling of burning logs in the fireplace. I sat next to my mother, and the chief began talking. "I see you're all prepared for bad news. Isabella identified your friend Inanna in our morgue. She was injured and was found dead on the stairs of the library early this morning."

Winter let a tear slide from her eye, and Raven clasped her hands together. Overall, neither of them looked particularly guilty to me.

My mother took my hand. "Can I get you some tea?" she asked.

"Please. And maybe some for Winter and Raven?"

She looked to the chief and he nodded. "Some for everyone."

She returned with a large tray full of mugs, a teapot, and a bottle of whiskey. "It's that kind of morning," she said. She quickly served us tea, only the police didn't take whiskey too.

"I'd like to break the questioning up into two groups. I'd like the Proctor family to stay here with me and everyone else to go with Officer Stanton."

Winter, Raven, and Hope stood and followed Kate out of the room. When they were gone, the chief had a hard glint in his eye. "Where are Thea and Delia?"

"At work," I answered. "Do you want me to call them?"

"No. I'll talk to them later." He set his mug down on the mantel. "Do you ladies realize how much trouble you could be in? Trouble I may not be able to get you out of."

"You don't think we're responsible for her death, do you?" Aunt Lily asked.

"That's just it, Lily. It doesn't matter what I think. Three women who have stayed here have died over the years, and that's going to trigger an in-depth investigation. If I don't start looking long and hard at all of you, it could mean my job."

Three women? Of course! Grandma's sister, my Great Aunt Jem, was killed by another houseguest we had when I was fourteen. Jemima, Hester, and now Inanna had all been guests at our house and were murdered.

"First, was she a witch?" the chief asked.

"She was. So are Hope, Winter and Raven, the women with Kate," Aunt Lily said.

"I thought so. You know I want to stay out of your business as much as possible, but I have to ask. Was there a good reason Inanna was killed?"

"Hold on there," Grandma said. "I don't like the direction this is going in. Are you asking if we had a good reason to kill her?"

"Settle down, Esther. I'm asking if she was the kind of woman people got angry at easily. Not necessarily whether you did it or not."

"I've only known her for a day, and she wasn't particularly nice to anyone," I said.

"Why was she here?" he asked.

I looked to Aunt Lily, who nodded. Okay, I'd tell him everything. "The women in my sorority don't want me in it. I can't leave, so we're not able to do our job. Inanna ran the California sorority, and Hope asked her for help. She came yesterday with Winter and Raven to do some training exercises with us."

"Who was at these exercises?"

"The seven women in my sorority, Inanna, Winter, and Raven. Ten of us altogether."

He rubbed his face. "That's a lot of suspects. Where's the rest of your sorority?"

"They went home last night. They were waiting for Hope to tell them to come back," I said.

"Okay. Let's call them back. Esther, can you do that?"

"Of course I can," she said.

"Good. Don't tell them why we need them back. And tell them to use the door—Kate's still here, but I'll reassign her as soon as I can. In the meantime, I want to talk to the women in the kitchen." He turned to me. "Isabella, I'd like you to come with me."

"Sure thing." I had no idea why he wanted me there, but I wasn't going to tell him no.

The chief and I sat at the kitchen table and he sent Kate to the living room. "First of all, I want you ladies to know that I've known about witches for a long time now. I know the Proctor women are witches, and I presume you are too."

Hope, Winter, and Raven looked to me. "It's true. Both the chief and Detective Palmer know. But not Officer Stanton," I said.

"Inanna would have flogged us if we ever even hinted at witchcraft to anyone," Winter said.

"Now that you know you can speak freely, I want you to tell me about your friend," the chief said.

Raven sat back and sighed. "She was highly dedicated to our sorority, and keeping us safe. That's why she was so strict about keeping our secrets."

The chief stood up and poured himself a glass of water. "Did she care for the witches in her sorority?"

"Absolutely," Winter and Raven said in unison.

I didn't believe that was true. "Chief, can I ask a question?"

He nodded to me.

"Last night, when we were doing our training exercise and got zapped—did she ever do that to you?"

I could see they didn't want to answer the question. "Did she have that spell cast on you at all times?"

Still no answer.

"What are you talking about?" the chief asked.

"Do you remember how I said my sorority didn't much like me? Inanna, Winter, and Raven came from California to help Hope get us to all work together. In last night's training exercise, if people didn't work well with the group, they got a small electric shock on the neck."

"They what now?" he asked.

"I got one, and it wasn't very strong. But they got stronger the more you didn't get along."

He turned from me to look at Winter and Raven. "Did she use this spell on you too?"

Both women looked uncomfortable and shifted in their seats.

"Would the spell die when she did?" the chief asked.

"We're not sure," Winter said.

"Can you try?" I asked. "We need to get to the truth quickly. Even if no one liked her, her murder shouldn't go unsolved."

"Inanna was mean to us," Raven said in a whisper.

After a moment she grinned. "Inanna was the meanest witch I ever knew."

"Once Inanna sucked you into the sorority, she ruled your whole life," Winter said.

"So, the spell died. I take it there are more of you in California with the same feelings for the victim?"

Winter smiled. "I can't believe the curse is gone. Probably all of us felt the same way."

"But we'd never have been able to do anything about it. The curse hurt far more if we imagined we wanted to hurt her," Raven said.

The chief stood up. "Thank you, ladies. We may have more questions for you later." He looked to me. "They can stay here until the investigation is over, right?"

"Absolutely."

"If you ladies would join us back in the living room?" the chief asked, though it wasn't really a question.

Once we were all together again, the chief began to talk. "We'll be treating this as a homicide for the time being. Detective Palmer will take the lead, and I expect each of you to fully cooperate with him. We'll find out what happened to your friend and, if she was murdered, we'll do our best to catch her killer."

CHIVE RIGHT IN

Chapter 6

Once Kate had taken everyone's information, she left for the station to check alibis. The New Hampshire sorority members, with the exception of Hope and me, left, grumbling about wasting their time going back and forth when it was clear they hadn't murdered anyone.

"Nice group you've got there," the chief said.

I frowned. "They're not my biggest fans. And none of them liked Inanna either."

Palmer knocked on the door and let himself in. I wanted to go to him and let him pull me into an embrace. I really needed him to tell me everything was going to be okay, because it didn't seem like it would be. Instead, I gave him a small smile.

"It's a heck of a case," the chief said. "Fifteen suspects here last night, not to mention anyone else she may have upset before yesterday."

Palmer's eyes widened. "Fifteen?"

"We had a meeting, and Inanna made a lot of people angry. Plus the rest of my family who were here," I said.

"Here's the thing, Palmer. I need to pass this off to you, and it needs to be by the book. This is the third murder related to the house, and we can't overlook anything. Never mind anything supernatural, you've got to follow the evidence where it leads."

Ignore the supernatural? In what was so obviously a supernatural killing? That didn't make sense to me. Maybe I'd have to investigate on my own.

"Yes, sir," was all Palmer said.

Once the chief left, I turned to Palmer. "You're not really going to ignore the supernatural, are you?"

He sat on the couch. "No. But any case I make has to be rooted firmly in the physical evidence, and with non-magic motives."

I put my hand on his. "Good. Because you can't just kill an old, strong witch without magic of your own."

He turned to look at me. "Oh yeah? What kind of magic are you thinking? Potions, spells, something else?"

"I can think of a few spells. I've read about a revenge spell that could work if a person were angry enough that murder seemed like the appropriate revenge. Maybe the killing curse of Marduk. I'm sure Grandma knows more than I do."

"How about potions?" he asked.

"Tons of potions would do the trick, but if we're thinking non-magically, there are a lot of poisons out there that most people could get their hands on. Has the coroner found evidence of poison?"

"I haven't heard anything. But we just declared this a murder, so he may not have had time to run any tests."

"She was definitely attacked. She's got a scorch mark across her face," I said.

"Are you up to seeing her again? I'd like to take a look," he said.

I nodded. The shock had worn off some, and I could see her again without my knees buckling.

"Good."

Once we climbed into his car, Palmer started to question me. "What is it about people staying at your house that gets them killed?"

I shook my head. "It's coincidence. Great Aunt Jem was killed for her grimoire, which is still missing. Her murderer was caught and was a friend of the family. Hester Johnson's murder was ordered by Jake Forster, and her murderers are in jail too. No relation to us, thankfully. As for Inanna, I don't know why she was killed, but I'm not surprised she had enemies. I'd bet everything I owned that no one in my family killed her. I don't know about Winter and Raven, though. Or anyone else from the California sorority."

We pulled into the hospital parking lot and parked. "Is it possible your house is cursed? People who stay there die?"

I pursed my lips. "Maybe? I wondered the same thing, but a curse would look different, I think. It would look more like accidents in the house, rather than murders outside the house."

He opened his door. "You probably shouldn't have people stay at the house anymore."

I got out of the car. "That's ridiculous."

He closed his door and we walked to the entrance of the building. "It probably doesn't matter. Once word gets out that people keep dying around the house, no one will want to stay."

He might have had a point there.

One of the coroners, Dr. Lucy Probst, was waiting for us as the elevator doors slid open.

"Lucy, meet Isabella Proctor. She consults on some of my weirder cases."

She held her hand out and we shook. "Nice to meet you."

"You too," I said.

"Were you able to find anything else on our victim?" Palmer asked.

"Let's talk in my office." She turned and we followed her to the office next to Max's. She didn't decorate her office like Max did. Lucy's office looked just like that—an office. She had a desk, several chairs, and a couch, but you could tell she didn't spend time sleeping in her office—it just didn't look lived in. She also didn't have a fridge or a treadmill. What she had was a set of lovely prints of anatomical sketches. You might not think they'd be attractive or artistic, but these were.

"Lovely prints," I said.

"Thank you. Please, have a seat," she said.

"Overall, I agree with Max. Your victim has an electrical burn on her face, which could have been accidental. At her age, that could be enough to disrupt her heart rhythm. I'd like to see the crime scene before I make a final ruling."

"She was found on the steps of the public library. Nothing there to cause that damage. I'll let you know when we find where this happened," Palmer said.

I shifted in my chair. "What would cause this kind of damage? Is there anything near the library?"

Lucy took a sip of her coffee. "Ugh, cold. Nothing within a few blocks, unless she climbed a telephone pole and was playing with the wires. Unlikely at her age."

There was a way for us to know where she was hurt, but it was a last resort. Thea's magic could tell her what happened to a person but, when she used it to see the last minutes of a person's life, it was deeply upsetting. After using it to exonerate my landlord's son at the end of last year, I vowed not to ask for her help unless it was absolutely necessary.

"We've got officers working a quarter-mile radius around the library looking for clues. Do you think she could have walked farther than that after sustaining her injury?" Palmer asked.

Lucy thought for a moment. "Unlikely at her age, but I can't rule out a surge of adrenaline keeping her going as she tried to find help. She didn't have any defensive wounds so, if this was an attack, she wasn't expecting it."

Palmer stood. "Thanks for your time, doctor. I'll let you know if we find anything else."

Back in the car, Palmer turned to me. "Tell me everything you know."

I bit my lip. "That's just it, I don't know anything. I don't know why she left the house that night, I have no idea if she was meeting someone, and I can't imagine where she might have been going. She lived in California for decades, so I don't think she still knew anyone around here. None of my sorority members seemed to know her."

"What about Winter and Raven? Would they have killed her?"

I thought about what they'd told the chief and me. "They didn't like her, that's for sure. But while she was alive, she had a spell over all her sorority members that they couldn't even say bad things about her, much less try to hurt her. The way Winter and Raven spoke, I think they'd have been too afraid to even try to hurt her."

Palmer's stomach growled. "I haven't eaten yet today. Do you want lunch?"

I nodded. "McGinty's?"

Once we were seated at the bar of McGinty's and had ordered our burgers, we started talking about the case again. "What we need is a good list of suspects."

I picked a pretzel out of the bowl between us. "Why are you so sure there are suspects? You don't think this was an accident?"

He took a sip of water. "Definitely not. I've been electrocuted, and you don't just walk for help. It puts you down, and you stay down for a while. Regardless of her additional powers, the body can only do so much. I'm convinced she was moved, and that means this wasn't an accident."

Some day I would ask about why he got electrocuted, but today we were too busy. "What about a Good Samaritan?"

"I doubt it. A person who wanted to help would have called the police, or brought her to the hospital."

Fair point. "I've got no one I can credibly point to. Everyone at the house and the rest of my sorority members ought to be investigated, but I can't think of any strong motives."

I bit my pretzel. "Both Hope and Grandma argued with Inanna, but not for anything worth killing over."

Palmer raised his eyebrows. "What did she and your grandmother have to argue about?"

I rolled my eyes and smiled. "Grandpa. Apparently Inanna tried to woo him away from Grandma a few weeks before they got married. Inanna said Grandma stole her only chance at happiness."

"And what did your grandmother say?" he asked.

"She said it was foolish to hold on to a grudge for so long, and that if Inanna had never found happiness, that was her own fault."

He nodded. "Did either of them threaten the other?"

I shook my head. "Grandma walked out, muttering about Inanna being an old fool."

Our burgers arrived and we ate in silence for a few minutes.

"What about Hope?" he asked.

"She didn't like the training methods. We got zapped when we didn't do what we were supposed to."

Palmer put his burger down. "Zapped? Like with a taser?"

"No. More like a shock from a dog fence. It wasn't nearly as painful as a taser."

He looked at me. "Are you okay? You weren't permanently hurt, were you?"

I put my hand on his arm. "No, I'm fine. We're all fine. I'm glad I don't have to deal with her training methods anymore though."

Palmer's phone beeped. He pulled it out and frowned at the text message he read. "I've got to go. Chief needs to see me."

I waved to the bartender. "Can we get these wrapped up?"

He pulled two plastic containers out from under the bar. "No problem. I don't think the detective has managed to finish a single lunch here without being called away."

"I'll drop you at home. I'd like to know what your family thinks about Inanna and if it was possible that she was murdered."

I'd rather go with him to see the chief, but he didn't invite me. I didn't see the text, so it might not even be about Inanna's murder. It stank to be cut out of parts of the investigation just because Palmer didn't think I needed to be there. On the other hand, there was no way I would beg him to include me in everything. I could find clues and murderers without him.

LISA BOUCHARD

Chapter 7

Surprisingly, no one was home when Palmer dropped me off at Proctor House. There was a note for me on the kitchen table telling me there would be a sorority meeting in an hour.

Even Jameson was gone, so I decided to practice teleportation out in the backyard. Even though Jameson said I'd made enough progress to practice on my own, I was still working with small objects. At least I wasn't always embedding them into the tables or walls anymore. I cast the cloaking spell over the yard and plucked a dry leaf from a tree. I set the leaf on the ground and made an X in the snow ten feet away. That was my goal. If I hit the target and the brittle leaf was intact, I would go in and make myself hot cocoa.

Who was I kidding? Even if I didn't get everything right, I'd make myself cocoa when I went in. But it wouldn't be victory cocoa.

I focused on the leaf and its destination. I closed my eyes and focused my intention on the leaf popping up on the X. Just as I released my intention to the leaf, a car horn blared on the street and I jumped. I knew before I opened my eyes that the leaf was nowhere near its target. I looked down to find a pulverized leaf in front of me. Jameson was right when he said it would be a long time before I was ready to work with anything living.

I plucked another leaf and tried again. I managed to get the leaf to appear fifteen feet from the target because nothing distracted me. The leaf wasn't crushed either. I took a deep breath and blew it out. This much focus was hard work, so I decided to go back inside.

Rather than make one mug of cocoa for myself, I made an entire saucepan full, so we'd all have some for the meeting. Maybe the warm, sweet drink would keep everyone's moods warm and sweet too. Hope and Grandma were the first to arrive, laden with bags from several stores in downtown Portsmouth. The aunts arrived next, home from work.

Aunt Nadia smiled when she saw me stirring a pot at the stove. "What are you making?"

"Hot cocoa. I did some teleportation practice and thought I deserved a treat. But I made enough for everyone."

Aunt Nadia gave me a hug while Aunt Lily pulled mugs down from the cabinet.

"Thanks. After the day I had, I could use some," my mother said.

The rest of the New Hampshire sorority blinked into existence next. Were they showing off because they knew I couldn't teleport yet? I put the thought aside. If they were showing off, I wasn't going to acknowledge it and, if they weren't, I wasn't going to seem impressed by them.

Winter and Raven arrived last, with bags of groceries. "We don't want to be a burden, or not contribute to the house," Winter said.

"I'd like to make dinner after our meeting," Raven said. "Have you ever had kimchi grilled cheese before?"

I hadn't, but that wasn't going to stop me from trying it. Maybe it was a good thing I hadn't finished my lunch. "Sounds interesting. I've never had kimchi before."

"It goes great with the ginseng chicken soup I'm going to make," Winter said.

Aunt Nadia ladled herself a mug of cocoa. "I guess I've got a night off. Thank you."

"All right, ladies. Let's get to our meeting first, then we'll worry about dinner."

We followed Hope into the living room, where a large whiteboard stood on an easel. "What's with the whiteboard?" Christina asked.

"Have a seat, everyone. We'll get to that in a minute."

We all sat and I was surprised to see Winter and Raven had joined us. Since Hope hadn't said anything, I assumed she wanted them there.

"I'd like to start by talking about Inanna for a moment. We all have our own opinions about her, but I think there are a few things we can all agree on. She was a strong woman, and a decisive leader. She took the California sorority, which was nothing more than several feuding factions, and turned it into a working, effective group of witches that saved a lot of lives and kept a lot of secrets in her tenure. "

I looked to Winter and Raven, who were both nodding.

Hope continued. "I think, having said that, we can agree her methods weren't always the kindest. I had no idea what she had planned for training us. All I knew was that I hadn't heard any complaints from her sorority members, and I assumed that meant all was well. I can only apologize to you, Winter and Raven, for that oversight. I won't make that mistake again."

I didn't think Hope should feel too bad. Who would have thought Inanna was using magic that skirted right up to the line of evil to keep her sorority in check? But like Hope said, we all knew better now.

"Having said all that, we still have work to do. We need to do whatever it takes to get over our differences and work together as a team. Finding Inanna's killer is the perfect opportunity for that. Since Raven and Winter need to stay in town, I hope they'll help guide us and share whatever they think will help find justice for Inanna."

"Of course we will," Winter said. "We didn't like her, but there's no way we can stand by as her murderer walks free."

"Agreed! The California sorority works well together, and we can show you how to do the same. I have some ideas about teambuilding exercises that I'd like to talk to you about," Raven said.

Sasha looked concerned. She was the person who was hurt the most during our previous training.

"Ideas that don't involve punishment," Raven said.

Hope smiled. "I'd like to hear them."

Jameson padded in. "I was listening at the door, and your priorities are wrong."

"How so?" Helen asked.

"My family is still alive, but not rescued. Finding Inanna's killer is important, but—and this is a big but—I think we need to work to save the living before we seek vengeance for the dead."

He had a good point there. "What do you want us to do?" I asked.

"I propose we go tonight, storm the house, and rescue all the familiars we can," he said.

That was a lot of speech for a room full of witches. He jumped into my lap and lay down. I scratched between his ears.

"I'm not sure that's the best plan," Hope said.

Jameson meowed.

"You were there just last night. They're going to be on their guard for another rescue attempt tonight. If we wait a day or two, they'll let their guard down."

Jameson hissed. "I don't think she'd say that if it were her family being held," he said to me.

I didn't think so either, but there wasn't much I could do about that. "I know. I promise we'll get them soon."

I couldn't help but look to Helen and Claire, who wanted their own familiars. I was sure they'd back me up when I insisted we rescue Jameson's sister soon.

"What did he say?" Hope asked.

"He's impatient to rescue his sister," I answered.

"Back to the issue at hand," Hope said. "The first thing we need to know is where Inanna went, what she was doing, and who she may have been meeting. Winter, Raven, do you have any ideas?"

We all turned to them. "Inanna lived in New Hampshire for a short time, decades ago. Maybe she went to visit old friends?"

I knew she'd lived in New Hampshire, because I overheard her arguing with Grandma. Grandma had laughed, saying Inanna never had a chance with Grandpa and it wasn't her fault that Inanna couldn't take the hint that he didn't want to see her anymore.

Inanna was furious. "He was about to propose to me, I knew he was. Did you use a confusion spell? Disguise yourself to look like me?"

Grandma sighed, and her tone remained calm. "I didn't trick him into anything. I didn't have to."

Grandma walked out of the living room, and I was pretty sure she saw me throw up a quick invisibility spell. Inanna walked out after her, but didn't see me.

"Grandma and Inanna had a fight the night she died," I said.

Everyone in the room turned to look at me. "What about?" Hope asked.

"Grandpa," I said.

"But he died years ago," Hope said.

I nodded. "I know. Inanna thought Grandma stole him away from her."

"Maybe that's why she moved to the other side of the country," Winter said.

"Okay, so we'll have to talk to Esther."

Raven stood. "If you want to know who might have wanted Inanna dead, I can give you a couple names."

Chapter 8

Who do you suspect?" Hope asked.

Jameson jumped off my lap and walked out of the room.

"Given what we just heard about the fight, I'd suggest looking into Inanna's ex-husband, Clive. If she was never happy with him, I can't imagine what a living nightmare she might have made his life," Raven said.

"Clive. Okay. What's his last name?" Hope asked.

"Clive Ouderkirk. He lives somewhere in New Hampshire. Now that I think of it, maybe she was going to visit him last night? You know, catch up and see how he's doing?"

I scoffed. "She didn't strike me as the sentimental type, but maybe."

"Okay, who else?" Hope asked.

"I didn't want to bring this up, because I know how much you care about him. But Jameson might have wanted to kill her. You know—"

"I beg your pardon?" I said. "You think my cat killed Inanna? With an electrical burn?"

"As I was saying, he wanted to protect his family. He knew how dire the familiar situation is in the rest of the country, and

I can only imagine he wouldn't want his family to be far from him."

No wonder people were angry that I had inherited Jameson. He wouldn't kill to keep them close, would he? As far as I knew, he hadn't killed any fraternity members in his rescue attempts, so I thought he wouldn't kill Inanna either. He had bigger things to worry about first.

"I don't see that happening," Claire said.

"Like I said, I didn't want to bring it up, but since we're trying to solve the crime, we need to look at everyone with any kind of motive."

At this point, Winter stood up. "You're pointing fingers at other people, but what about yourself? You hated the control Inanna had over you and, since we learned her spell died with her, you've had nothing but bad things to say about her."

Raven looked stunned. "Of course I have. I've got years of resentment to get off my chest. And what about you? You can't have been any happier than I was."

"I wasn't. But I know I don't resort to violence. I'm not so sure about you."

Hope moved between the two women before it came to blows, magical or otherwise. "Ladies! Please. Let's settle down and stop accusing every person we can think of." She turned to Raven. "Do you have any other credible suspects?"

Raven shook her head and sat down. "What about you, Winter?"

"No. Raven already said the ones I thought of."

"Okay then. Let's start with the people here at the house. We can talk to Esther and Jameson in the morning. Right now, I don't think we're in any state to work together."

CHIVE RIGHT IN

We left the living room; the New Hampshire sorority members went home while Winter, Raven, and I stayed behind.

After an oddly delicious dinner, I decided to go home. The tension at Proctor House was starting to get to me, and I really wanted to be in my own bed, with my own things, and wake up not worrying about what was going on around me.

Jameson didn't come home until after I went to bed, so I didn't get to tell him about my practice in the backyard. As I drifted off to sleep, I made a mental note to remember to tell him in the morning.

The next morning, I felt more refreshed than I had for days. I didn't worry about witches arguing in the hallway, who was plotting to accuse whom, nothing. Jameson jumped up on my bed. "I hear I was accused of killing Inanna last night."

I frowned. "You were, but not in any real, credible way. It's just because they don't know you and think you'd kill to protect your family. I can see where they think that. But if you haven't done it so far, you wouldn't start now, would you?"

Jameson said nothing.

"You haven't killed anyone recently, have you?"

"Not in the last two decades. If the problem starts to require killing, it's a failure on my part for not taking care of it sooner."

I breathed a sigh of relief. What he did before I was even alive wasn't any of my business, and I wasn't going to ask.

"Are you ready for another exciting day of witchcraft?" I asked him.

He sneezed and rubbed his nose. "We're not doing witchcraft. You're holding meetings where you point your fingers at each other instead of using your gifts to figure out who killed Inanna."

He was right. No wonder I was dreading going back to Proctor House today. "They're going to question you today, if you show up there."

He stretched in the patch of sunlight streaming through my window. "I know. I considered avoiding them, but the sooner I clear my name, the sooner they'll be willing to help me."

"So we grab breakfast, check in at the apothecary, and head over. Deal?"

"Deal. And, Isabella . . ."

"Yes?"

He jumped off the bed. "Never mind. I was being overly sentimental."

Overly sentimental? Jameson? That was a first. What was he going to say? The only thing that made sense was he was happy I'd be there with him. I was glad, too. It would be better for him to have a friend in his corner.

I opened the door to my apothecary, a little nervous because I'd left the sales floor in Mackenzie's hands for several days in a row.

"Good morning, Isabella," she said from the tea table. "I thought you weren't scheduled to be back until tomorrow at the earliest."

I hadn't been, but I felt odd not being there every day. "I'm just checking in, making sure you don't need anything. I've got family stuff to deal with today, so I don't have much time."

She finished making tea and walked back to the counter. "Mrs. Olivera wants you to make her more arthritis ointment. She says it works great, and she's going to send the women in her bridge club to get some as well."

I smiled. There was no greater compliment than being recommended by a happy customer. "When did you tell her to come for it?"

"I sold her the last one we had, so you've got a week. Unless her bridge club comes in before then. But I can always take orders and let you know."

I nodded. It took about an hour to make the ointment, but I didn't have the time this morning. "I'll be in as soon as I can to make a double batch. Anything else happen that I should know about?"

She pursed her lips. "Alex, the guy who sleeps out back, he's been in every day asking for you. No emergency, I think he's lonely and just wanted to talk. We're starting to have tea every morning, and he's telling me stories about when he was younger."

"Thank you. I'll see him before I go."

I took a quick look at the bookkeeping software on my office computer and saw that sales were doing well. I loved running a business that provided for me, but the downside was that I needed to devote more time to making my products. Just as soon as we catch Inanna's killer, I promised myself, I'll spend a week restocking everything.

I walked out back to see Alex coming out of his tent. "Good morning. I hear you've been asking for me."

He smiled as he rolled up his sleeping bag. "Nothing urgent. Just wondered where you got off to."

"A woman that was staying at my grandmother's house was murdered. I'm helping Detective Palmer find the killer."

His eyebrows furrowed. "Not sure I like the sound of that. What if you find the murderer and he's dangerous? What if he tries to kill you too?"

"I almost always investigate with other people, so I'm not alone. Detective Palmer does a really good job keeping me safe too. I trust him with my life."

Alex laughed. "That's because you're in love with him. Love makes a woman, or a man, do stupid things sometimes." He put his sleeping bag on the ground and began to disassemble his tent. "Be careful."

"I will. Are you going somewhere?" I asked.

"No. But I don't leave my things unattended for the day. I carry them around with me."

I didn't want to intrude by asking more questions about how he chose to lead his life. "How are you doing? I hear you and Mackenzie are having tea in the mornings."

"Nice girl, but she won't take no for an answer. Once she realized I was the night watchman, she felt obligated to feed me breakfast. Kept telling me she had too much food, you weren't here, and it would go to waste." He shrugged. "What could I do? I took it. Now we have breakfast most mornings."

"I'm glad you're here, keeping an eye on her too. Thank you."

He put his tent in its bag and zipped it up. "It's nice here, and you two don't make too much of a fuss over me." He slung his backpack over his shoulder. "Well, I'm off for the day. Maybe I'll see you tomorrow."

I watched as he walked away, wondering how he came to be so happy in a life many people would find miserable.

I didn't find an answer on the brisk walk to Proctor House, then put him out of my mind. There was a lot to do today, and I didn't think any of it would be pleasant.

Jameson jumped down from the chestnut tree in the front yard as I walked up the driveway. "Took you long enough," he said.

"I had to check in at the apothecary, then I had a little chat with Alex. But I'm here now, so we might as well go in and get it over with."

Chapter 9

As soon as I opened the kitchen door, I heard yelling from the dining room. Jameson and I rushed in to see what the problem was. Winter and Raven were on one side of the table, and Grandma was on the other. I could feel unspent magic crackling in the air.

"Hey! Cut it out! You're not going to hex each other, so just drop your spells right now."

To my relief, they did.

"Since when am I, the youngest here, the voice of reason? Really, you three ought to be ashamed of yourselves. Now sit down and tell me what's going on."

"Your grandmother—" Winter started.

"It's my house, so I'll fill in my granddaughter," Grandma interrupted. "These two wanted to use a truth spell on me. Claimed they couldn't trust me to tell the truth."

My eyes widened. We'd all been known to stretch the truth, but to try forcing a truth spell on her, in her own home, was too much to believe. "You can't force her to do anything. Hasn't your time with Inanna taught you anything?"

"But—" Raven said.

"I don't even know any truth spells. Do you?"

Raven looked sheepish. "Inanna knew several. I watched her closely enough that I think I can replicate at least one of them."

I was astonished. "First of all, there are several of them? Second of all, you were going to experiment on my grandmother? That's unacceptable. I'll tell you what we're going to do. We're going to wait until Hope arrives, then you can question my grandmother. Without any spells."

Winter and Raven looked disappointed. "Fine. But if she's guilty, we're bringing her to the California sorority for punishment."

I looked to Grandma, who didn't seem the least bit worried. "That okay with you, Grandma?"

"Since I didn't do it, sure. But if these two fools overstep again, I can't promise to be kind to them until they get back in line."

"Grandma, can I see you in the kitchen?" I asked.

Once we were in the kitchen, I cast a silencing spell around us. "Why did you let the situation get so bad?"

Grandma scoffed. "Those two? I've got more magic in my little toe than they were threatening to throw at me. I don't think there's anything they can do that I can't defend." She pulled out a chair and sat. "Besides, I didn't kill Inanna. Why would I? It's not like she was coming after my husband again. She was angry with me, but I hadn't even given her a thought over the last forty years."

"She didn't say anything to get under your skin? Nothing to provoke you?" I asked.

"You're taking them seriously, aren't you?" she asked.

"Of course I am. I know as much as you do that you didn't kill Inanna, but think about it from their point of view. All they know is how angry she was. Now they find out it was all because of you, and they have the smallest idea of why, and it's hard not to imagine you felt the same way. If we let them see your side, they'll lighten up on you and move on to better suspects."

She rolled her eyes. "Yeah, like your cat."

"One battle at a time," I said. "Let me get you off the hook, then I'll worry about Jameson."

She smiled up at me. "How'd you get to be so sensible?"

"Not from you, that's for sure. I'm dismissing the silencing spell, and we'll just wait here for Hope."

We didn't have to wait long before Hope was knocking at the door. I let her in. "You could have just appeared inside."

She shook her head. "That's rude." She took one look at Grandma. "What's wrong?"

"Winter and Raven have decided I must be a murderer, and they were trying to use a truth spell on me."

Hope blanched. "Those are . . . illegal."

Illegal? I didn't think we had laws outside of harm no one. Obviously, some people didn't hold to that one though. "If they're illegal, who is in charge of making sure they're not used?"

"The head of each sorority is responsible for the behavior of her group. We don't force people to do things they don't want here. Maybe it's different in California."

Or maybe now that there was no head of the sorority, it was a free-for-all.

"When I walked in, they were in a standoff. I brought Grandma in here so they could all cool off."

"Esther, you know how this works. We've got to ask you questions. I promise no one will use any spells on you. Can we finish this up quickly so we can get to finding the real killer?"

Grandma stood up. "Fine. Let's get this charade over with."

Winter and Raven were surprised to see us back in the dining room.

"Ask away," Grandma said.

Winter asked the first question. "What was the issue between you and Inanna?"

Grandma leaned forward in her seat. "When we were much younger, Inanna and I were friends. She lived in Portsmouth, and we had the same mentor for our spell work. We met my husband when he delivered furniture to our mentor."

Grandma smiled at the memory. "He was a handsome man, and we both flirted outrageously with him. The poor guy had no idea what was going on."

My grandmother flirted? Outrageously? I had a hard time seeing that.

"We turned it into a contest, and Inanna lost. She never got over it."

"Wait a minute," I said. "You married Grandpa because you won him in a contest?"

"That's not why we married. Once he chose me over Inanna, I gave him plenty of opportunities to walk away, but by that time he was head over heels in love with me."

I felt a little better that the one strong marriage I knew wasn't built on a sham.

"Then what happened?" Raven asked.

"Inanna couldn't hide her anger at me, and our friendship died. By the time he and I married, she had already married Clive out of spite. When that marriage ended badly and she was packing to leave for California, our mentor told her not to go until she'd worked through her feelings for us. He warned her if she didn't, she'd carry the burden of anger for the rest of her life."

Raven leaned back in her chair. "I can attest that she was angry for all the time I knew her. She never mentioned you though."

"I had no idea she still held that grudge. I would never have invited her here if I did," Hope said.

"Do you think she came to exact some sort of warped justice on you?" Raven asked.

Grandma shook her head. "No. She was still angry with me, but I got the sense she was focused on the sorority."

I wasn't sure about that. "She seemed to have it in for me. Now I know why. She focused her anger on me instead of you, maybe because I was an easier target."

"Did she provoke you into some sort of fight or duel?" Winter asked.

"No. I know better than to let my emotions run away with me that much," I said. Okay, I lied about not letting my emotions get the better of me. But we hadn't fought.

Winter frowned at me. "You'd never survive a duel with Inanna. I was speaking to Esther."

I blushed. Of course I wouldn't have survived fighting her.

Grandma patted my knee. "Who do you think taught Isabella her self-control? When I saw Inanna, I saw a sad, lonely, defeated woman. Why would I fight her? In every way that matters, I'd already won."

Hope stood up. "Does this convince you Esther didn't kill Inanna?"

"Not yet," Raven said. "Where were you the night she was murdered?"

Grandma rolled her eyes. "I was here. Half the night I was in the kitchen, with you. Once I said I was going to bed, that's exactly what I did. I fell sound asleep. I didn't hear her go out, and I didn't follow her anywhere."

"Who says she went anywhere? She could have been murdered here and moved to the library after," Winter said.

I shook my head. "Do you think no one would have heard that kind of magic being thrown around? A witch as strong as she was wouldn't let someone get close enough to hurt her. The burn had to be magical, and we'd have all felt that."

Winter looked like she didn't want to believe me but, after a moment, conceded. "I suppose you're right. Fine. I'm willing to say it's highly unlikely Esther killed Inanna. But that doesn't mean the rest of you are in the clear."

Grandma stood up. "About time you got to that conclusion. I've got things to do with my day, so I'm leaving."

As she walked out, I turned back to our inquisitors. "What do you mean the rest of us aren't in the clear? Now who do you want to question?"

Before they said anything, I knew they meant me.

"You'd have motive. Inanna looked like a threat to your family, and you might have decided to take matters into your own hands, get in a lucky spell, and remove Inanna before she could harm your grandmother."

"What in the blazing cauldrons are you talking about?" my mother said from the doorway.

I turned to her. "Mom? How long have you been there?"

"Not long. But long enough to know this is a ridiculous waste of everyone's time." She walked into the room and stood in front of Winter and Raven. "We know how to solve murders in this family. Goddess knows it's not a skill I wanted us to have, but she clearly had other intentions for us. You want to know who killed Inanna? So do we. I suggest you sit back and let Isabella and Palmer do their thing."

"But, but—" stammered Winter.

"Or we'll ask you to leave."

I drew in a sharp breath. Asking witches to leave your house once they'd been invited in was shockingly rude. Even threatening it was not something we did.

"Quit playing amateur detective, and let them do their work. In the meantime, I suggest you see some of the tourist attractions and enjoy the rest of your time here."

Before they could say anything else, my mother turned and left. I didn't want to deal with the aftermath of her threat, so I followed her and went back to the apothecary.

CHIVE RIGHT IN

Chapter 10

I felt a little bad for leaving Hope to deal with the indignant California witches, but not enough to stay. By the time I got to the apothecary, I'd shed the weight of Grandma being a suspect. And you know what? My mother was right. Palmer and I were experts at finding killers. No one would be surprised he was, but me? Twenty-one-year-old shop owner with hardly any real-life experience? I was an expert.

"I'm back," I called out as I opened the apothecary door. Mackenzie was dusting shelves and humming to herself.

"Hi. I wasn't expecting to see you again today."

"Neither was I, but my day freed up and I thought I'd get a head start on the arthritis ointments."

I hung my coat and bag in my office and got right to work in the prep room. I missed making potions and serving my customers. I missed chatting with Mackenzie when the work was all done. Maybe after we found Inanna's killer, I'd have some time off from murder investigations and could fully reimmerse myself in my business.

I assembled and gently warmed the ingredients for the arthritis ointment. The green, earthy scent of the eucalyptus had me wishing for spring. It would be here soon enough and then I'd start to miss the brisk mornings when the ground was covered with a fresh coating of snow. I felt like it was time for a walk in a forest to reconnect to Mother Earth. Maybe Palmer and I could do that once we solved the case.

Once I poured the ointment into jars, I took a slow walk around the apothecary to see what else I needed to make. Bubble bath, of course, hair tonic, ginger digestive tincture, and almost all the scented candles needed to be restocked. I would need to order more supplies to finish some of these, but I could at least get to work on the bubble bath and the candles.

As I was melting a five-pound block of candle wax, I decided to fill Jameson in on a few things.

Hey, are you busy?

Not so much I can't talk.

Good. First off, you're not a suspect in Inanna's murder anymore. Second, did you know she used a spell to keep her witches under control?

I could practically feel his eye roll through our connection.

Of course I'm not a suspect. And I'm not surprised she had to resort to extreme measures. She never struck me as a strong leader.

Where are you?

I'm at Chandler House, listening to a meeting.

What? Jameson, that's not safe. Get out of there before they see you.

I figured out what to do. I can't be invisible, but I can have a glamour. I look like a spider, and I'm hiding on the underside of a chair. No one will see me.

I had to admit, that was a good hiding place. *How did you even get in the building?*

I've been poking around all day in the museum areas, looking for anything I can find on the fraternity.

Did you find anything?

No. That's when I decided to sneak into the private areas on the third floor.

Okay, so what's going on?

They're talking about the power vacuum in California and how they need to get out there right away.

What? They aren't there already? I thought they were a larger group with people everywhere.

Apparently not. Have Winter and Raven told their sorority that Inanna is dead?

I had no idea. I assumed they had, but I never asked. *Unknown. I'll ask though.*

I'll stay a little longer and see if I hear anything else important.

Be careful, Jameson, they already hurt you once this week. And have you seen your sister? Is she okay?

I don't dare go near her. Hope was right, we need to give them time to let their guard down.

He broke the connection, and I took the wax off the hotplate. So much for making more candles.

Mackenzie looked confused when I grabbed my coat and bag. "Leaving so soon?"

I rolled my eyes. "Family stuff. I swear there's always one drama or another."

She laughed. "Tell me about it. Maybe I'll see you tomorrow."

Maybe. But I couldn't promise anything.

I started to walk to Proctor House when I realized we told Winter and Raven to go do touristy things for the day. Where would I find them?

Rather than trying to hunt them down, I attempted telepathy. *Winter, where are you?* I had no idea if either of them could answer me back, but it was worth a try. *Raven, can you hear me?*

My cell phone rang. I fished it out of my bag and saw a number with an 818 area code. Was that California? "Hello?"

"Is that you with the unholy screaming in my head?" Raven asked.

"Maybe? I was trying to contact you. I didn't have your number to call."

Raven took a deep breath. "You do now, so use it from now on. What do you want?"

I started walking back to the apothecary. "Jameson wanted to know if you told the other California sorority members that Inanna was dead. He's listening in to a fraternity meeting, and they're talking about the power vacuum in your state."

"Cauldrons and kitten tails," she cursed. "Everyone must know, because her spells have lifted. As for what they're doing, I have no idea. Winter and I need to go back right away."

"Palmer told you not to leave town though."

"We'll let him know how to get in touch with us."

She hung up before I had the chance to say anything else. Palmer wasn't going to be happy about them going home, but I doubted he'd force them to return.

Anything else going on? I asked Jameson.

They're congratulating themselves for being clever.

Winter and Raven are leaving for home now. With any luck, they can prevent the fraternity from taking control.

They did what? They promised to help with the rescue mission. You'll need to call them back when we're ready to move.

I'd forgotten about their promise of assistance. *Hope will get in touch with them.*

My phone rang with Palmer's ringtone. "Hey, what's up?"

"The chief is forcing me to take the night off. Something about exceeding the maximum hours worked in a week. Do you have plans?"

"I was thinking about going for a walk in the woods. Want to join me?"

"I'd love to. Pick you up at six?"

I smiled. An actual date where he wasn't allowed to work. "I'll be at my apartment."

Chapter 11

I Instead of heading back to Proctor House, I went to my apartment. The first thing I did was sit on my couch and relax, focusing on a lit meditation candle. I didn't want to have my mind still wrapped up in the case when it was time to focus on Palmer and the forest.

Once I felt relaxed, I changed into warm clothes and prepared a thermos of hot cocoa for us.

He knocked on my door promptly at six. "Did you check the peephole before you opened the door?" he asked as I let him in.

"You know how I put a ward on your house to help keep you safe? My apartment has the same thing, but stronger. If you wanted to hurt me, you wouldn't be able to come in."

He helped me get into my long stadium coat. "True. But what happens when you're not at home and forget to look? It's not good to become complacent."

I zipped my coat. "You're probably right."

"You didn't tell me which forest you wanted to walk in, so how does the Rye town forest sound?"

I'd been there in the summer before, but never in winter. The paths were wide and we wouldn't need to worry about getting lost. "It's beautiful, I'd love to go there."

I grabbed the thermos and we drove the fifteen minutes to Rye, managing not to talk about murders or suspects.

"I brought flashlights and hand warmers," he said as he pulled them out of his trunk.

He was definitely not used to dating a witch yet. The question was, do we use his equipment or do I just cast a spell? "You know what never runs out of batteries?" I asked.

He looked confused. "Solar powered lights?"

I cast a spell and created a small ball of light over my hand. "And it can be as large as we want once we're out of sight of the road."

He put the flashlights back in his trunk. "Have you got a warming spell too?"

I nodded. "Sure do. And they're both easy enough that I can hold them at the same time."

He held his hand out to me. "Let's go then."

We walked to the entrance of the forest. "Is there anything special you need to do here?" he asked.

"Like a ritual? No. I just wanted to spend some time in nature, out of the city. If we see anything beautiful, we can stop to admire it though."

I cast a warming spell over the two of us. Palmer grinned. "That feels amazing. It's like I'm warm from the inside out, and the weather doesn't have a chance to affect me."

I let the light get larger and we continued walking. "I had a nice time at the New Year's Eve party."

"Even with Mikey getting drunk and making a fool of himself?"

I hadn't liked that part of the evening so much, but mostly because I felt Kate's embarrassment like it was my own. "Maybe not that part so much. The dancing was fun."

Palmer pulled me closer to him. "The dancing was fun."

"And dessert was fun. I can't believe both Kate and I ate more than you did."

He laughed. "If I'd known there was going to be a contest, I wouldn't have eaten so much dinner."

We continued walking until we got to the main clearing. Moonlight streamed down and sparkled on the snow. I extinguished my light and stood silently for a moment. Beauty like this brought me closer to nature, closer to my true purpose of helping others any way I could.

I put my arm around Palmer and leaned into him. At that moment there was nothing else in the world I wanted.

"I'd sell my house in a heartbeat if I could find one that gave us this view at night," Palmer said.

I looked up at him. "You don't like your house?"

"It's not the house, it's the location. A city neighborhood will never be as beautiful as this. Proctor House comes close, but a detective would never be able to afford something like that."

He sounded sad. "You don't think you need to have a huge house to impress me, do you?"

"I can't ask you to settle for something as small as my house. Not when you're used to . . ."

I nudged him with my arm. "I'm used to a four-room apartment. And if I wasn't already impressed with you, I wouldn't be here right now."

He bent down and kissed me. For as much time as we spent together, we hadn't kissed more than a few times. This kiss promised there would be a lot more in our future.

I grinned up at him. "Very impressive, Detective Palmer."

"Should we keep walking?" he asked.

Clouds obscured half the full moon and the wind was picking up. "We should head back. A storm is coming in."

Fat flakes of snow started falling on our way back to the car. I bent down and grabbed a handful of snow. Behind my back, I made a snowball and threw it at Palmer. I wasn't a good shot, and I barely hit his shoulder.

"Hey!" he yelled as he bent down to grab snow. "No fair attacking an unarmed man."

Palmer had much better aim than me, and he hit me mid-torso.

I ran to the car and hid behind it. "Truce!"

He laughed and unlocked the car. "Get in, troublemaker. You know, I could arrest you for assaulting a police officer."

I laughed. "I dare you to try. One call to Grandma or Aunt Lily, and you'd regret that move for the rest of your life."

He grimaced. "True. I'll let it slide. This time."

Before we turned onto the road, he stopped the car and looked at me. "I'd like your help with something."

"You're not supposed to be working tonight. Whatever it is, we can do it tomorrow."

He frowned. "It's not work related. Mostly."

All trace of joking had left his voice and this concerned me. "Of course. What do you need?"

"I haven't been able to go back to the Crispy Biscuit since we closed Dan's case."

I put my hand on his and squeezed. "That's understandable. It was a horrible day for you."

"But I can't continue like that. What if I need to go for work? I can't have a mental block about the building. I won't be able to do my job right if I do."

I nodded. I didn't have anything to ease his memories, but I could make something to ease his tension. Oddly, my intuition didn't see any potions I needed to make for him. "What can I do?"

"Can we go there to eat? Right now?"

"Of course we can." He pulled out of the parking lot and drove us to the restaurant. I hadn't been back there for a while either. I had opportunities, but I'd always found another place to go. This dinner would be good for both of us.

Before he opened the door to the Crispy Biscuit, he took a deep breath. "I'm not sure how well I'm going to do in there."

"We can leave if you need to, but why don't we take it one step at a time. Let's just open the door and step in."

I took his hand as he opened the door. We walked in together and were greeted by a smiling Emma.

"Isabella, Detective. How nice to see you. Table for two?"

"Ah, yes," he said.

She picked up two menus and looked at the seating chart. "Problem. The only tables I have left are close to the table you had last time you were here."

I admired her tact. The "last time you were here" was so much nicer than "the table your cousin was murdered at."

He squeezed my hand and I squeezed back, ready to do whatever he was ready for. "That's fine. The same table would be fine."

Without another word, she brought us to our table and left us with menus. "I'll be back in a minute to take your order."

He glanced at the menu then put it down.

"You okay?" I asked.

"Do you have any food allergies?"

I shook my head. "No. And I'll check all our food for poisons if you want me to."

"I'd like that."

I didn't tell him that my senses naturally broke down the ingredients in foods, drinks, perfumes, and other potions. He didn't need to know it took effort sometimes to taste food like everyone else did, instead of tasting the individual ingredients.

He still didn't look relaxed, and I thought he might bolt any second now.

I took his hand. "Want to hear a story?"

He nodded.

I cast a quick silencing spell before I started. "When I was six, I was convinced I was going to be the best witch ever. But everyone told me I needed to work hard, so I decided to start practicing."

He nodded. "Sounds reasonable."

"Sure, if I wanted to be a mathematician. Casting spells at that age is dangerous, because kids don't know what they're doing, and their intentions are all over the place."

"Did you even know any spells that young?"

Emma dropped off our water and I released the spell. "Have you decided what you want?"

I hadn't even looked at the menu. "Can I get a cheeseburger and curly fries?"

"Absolutely. Lettuce and tomato?"

"Yes please. And can I get a ginger ale to drink?"

She wrote my order down and looked to Palmer. He looked like he was losing his nerve. "Maybe something light? Soup?" I suggested.

"Chicken noodle and ginger ale for me too."

Emma patted his shoulder. "You're doing great. I'll bring your food over in a couple minutes."

I recast the silencing spell. "She's right. You're doing great. Want to hear the rest of my story?"

He looked to his water. "Is this okay?"

I had checked it the instant Emma set it on the table, but I took another moment to double check. "Yes, it's fine."

He picked the glass up and brought it to his lips, but didn't drink.

"So, I was going to be the best witch ever, even though I didn't know any spells. Grandma left a beginner's spell book out where I could reach it and I took it. I read it, hiding under my bed, until I had those spells memorized. Then I put the book back so no one knew I'd taken it."

"This isn't going to be good, is it?" he asked.

"It's hilarious now, but then . . . not so much. I don't know how you were when you were six, but I wasn't afraid of anything, and the idea of starting off small and working my way up to a larger spell didn't occur to me. That weekend I got up early on Saturday morning and started practicing the invisibility spell on myself."

His eyes grew wide. "You didn't."

I nodded. "Sure, I could have made anything invisible, but I picked myself. After the third try, it worked. I couldn't see myself in the mirror, and anything I picked up turned invisible too."

Emma returned with our drinks and some crackers. "Food will be out soon, and I thought you'd like these with your soup."

Silencing spell went down, we said thanks, then it went back up again.

"The crackers are fine to eat, too."

Palmer opened a package and took the tiniest nibble. "So there you were, invisible on a Saturday morning. What happened next?"

"I walked around, being as quiet as I could, thinking I was the most amazing witch of all time." I took a deep breath, remembering the scary part. "Until my mother started to look for me. It turns out I'd cast a cloaking spell instead, and she couldn't see me or hear me."

"Did you drop the spell and tell her what you did?" he asked.

"I couldn't. I didn't know how to. I couldn't even remember the name of the spell. I sat on the couch, crying, thinking I'd be like a ghost forever."

He squeezed my hand. "That must have been terrifying for you."

I nodded. "In the end, Grandma came to the rescue. I hadn't been as sneaky with the spell book as I thought. She performed a complicated series of spells to remove every spell in the house. I popped back into sight, and I'd never been so happy to be in trouble in all my life."

"How many spells does your house have?" he asked.

"Oh, lots. I can think of at least a dozen permanent ones off the top of my head."

"Did your grandmother learn her lesson about leaving her books around for you to read?"

"I don't know. I'm not sure she had to. When the aunts reinstated all the spells, they enchanted a bookshelf and put all the books my cousins and I were not allowed to read on it. The books felt glued onto the shelf to us, and we couldn't pull them off."

"Did you get punished?" he asked.

"Not really. It was obvious nothing my mother could do would teach me more than the lesson I'd already learned. I think I wasn't allowed to have dessert for a week, but everyone turned a blind eye when Thea and Delia snuck me some. But I'll tell you, I never opened that book again, I was too afraid of what else I might do to myself."

Emma brought our dinner. "Here you go. Let me know if you need anything else."

I checked his soup and nodded. "Go ahead."

He took a spoonful, looked at it suspiciously, then ate it.

"Not to make it sound like you're a three-year-old, but good job eating your soup."

"I think I'm over the worst of it," he said. "Thank you."

I put ketchup on my plate and dipped a fry in it. "You're welcome. Thank you for trusting me to take care of you."

He reached his hand across the table and took mine. "You do more than that, you know. You see things differently than I do."

I gave his hand a squeeze. "I should hope so, we're very different people."

"Are you free tomorrow morning? I'd like you to come with me to talk to Clive."

I thought for a moment. "I've really got to get to the shop tomorrow. Can we go early?"

Chapter 12

Palmer picked me up promptly at seven the next morning to speak to Clive, Inanna's ex-husband. "You ready?"

I put my coat on. "You bet."

"Thank you again for last night. I don't think I'd have made it without you."

I took his hand in mine. "You're welcome."

"Was that story you told me true?"

I laughed. "Every regrettable moment of it. I don't think I could have made up something like that on the spot."

In the car, he handed me coffee and a small white bag. "Pastry?"

He winked at me. "I know how to bribe people who help me early in the morning."

"Excellent. I work better with"—I opened the bag—"éclairs. I checked with Grandma last night, and she said Clive was a strange guy."

"What kind of strange?" he asked as he pulled out of my parking lot.

"Grandma said he was strange even for a witch. But not dangerous. Just . . . not like us."

"I looked him up early this morning, and he's married with two kids. Seems normal to me."

I bet I seemed normal to him the first time he met me too.

"He's an accountant, his wife is a chiropractor. You'd never know he'd once been married to a witch."

"Or that he was a witch himself. Grandma told me when she and Grandpa got engaged, Inanna demanded Clive marry her the day before Grandma's wedding."

"The day before?" Palmer asked.

"Inanna thought everyone would be talking about her wedding at Grandma's. And they were—but only to compare the two ceremonies and receptions, and Grandma's were better."

"Ouch! That's got to hurt."

Palmer pulled up to a gray colonial and turned the car off. "Do you expect any trouble from him?"

"No. But I'll be ready, just in case."

Palmer knocked on the front door and a man in his mid-seventies answered. He'd lost the battle to male pattern baldness, and his shaved head shined in the morning sunlight. "Can I help you?"

Palmer flashed his badge. "I'm Detective Steve Palmer and this is my associate, Isabella Proctor."

Clive's eyes widened at my name. "Proctor?"

I nodded. "You may know my grandmother, Esther."

Color drained from his face. "I used to. But I've given up that life."

I scowled at him. He should know better than to even hint at being a witch.

"If we could talk inside, sir?" Palmer asked.

Reluctantly, Clive let us in. "My wife doesn't know anything."

"And we're happy to keep it that way, as long as you cooperate," I said.

Clive led us to his study. "We can speak privately here. Please, sit."

We sat in the two leather armchairs that flanked the fireplace. Absent-mindedly, Clive snapped his fingers and the fireplace roared with a crackling fire.

I cleared my throat. I did not like the way he was ignoring witch safety rules. "If you could refrain from magic in front of non-witches."

He looked up at us. "What? Oh, those foolish rules." He snapped his fingers again and the fire went out.

"Stop that! You have no idea what Detective Palmer does and doesn't know. Just follow the safety rules, please."

Clive looked confused. "He didn't even flinch when I started the fire. Of course he knows what we can do. When you get to be as old as I am, you get a feel for who can handle knowing the truth. The detective can handle it. My wife, no way."

Palmer cleared his throat. "Could you tell us the last time you saw your ex-wife?"

"Why do you ask?" Clive asked.

"We're investigating her death. Answer the question, please."

Clive's face drained, and it hadn't regained all its color back from meeting us at the door. Palmer stood. "Please, have a seat."

Clive sat and put his head in his hands. "Inanna's dead?"

"Yes," I said.

"She came to see me three days ago. She stayed for ten minutes, then left," Clive said.

Palmer pulled out his notebook. "Did she visit you often?"

Clive shook his head. "I haven't seen her since the divorce, decades ago."

I could think of a million answers to my question, but I asked it anyway. "Why did you get divorced?"

He chuckled. "She hated my lack of ambition. I never wanted to make a name for myself in the community. I just wanted to study, learn, and develop stronger magic. Not to use, mind you, but just to see how far the limits of our abilities could be pushed."

"It seems strange that she'd pick this week to visit you. What was the purpose of her visit?" Palmer asked.

He stood up and walked to a tall metal filing cabinet. "When I was much younger, I was quite good at creating hexes." He pulled open the middle drawer and pulled out a folder. "She wanted my sleeping hex."

He tried to hand the folder to Palmer, but I jumped up and snatched it out of his hand. This man was a danger to witches, and I needed to talk to Hope about him once this case was over. "I'll take that. Honestly, you need to be more careful. I'm amazed your wife doesn't know anything."

"What did she want the sleeping hex for?" Palmer asked.

Clive looked at him like he was an idiot. "To put people to sleep."

"Which people," Palmer said, all friendliness gone from his voice.

"She didn't say, and I didn't ask. I don't like being blackmailed, and the sooner I got her out of my house, the happier I knew I'd be."

I looked through the hexes in the file. My blood ran cold when I saw the evil magic he'd written out and had almost handed to Palmer. "Did she take any other hexes?"

"No. All she wanted was the sleeping hex. Can I ask, how did she die? And are you sure she's really dead?"

My heart sank. What if she was just sleeping and not dead? If the hex backfired on her, would the coroner be able to tell she was still alive?

"Our coroners do a thorough test for signs of life before an autopsy. Yes, she was definitely dead. Other than that, I can't comment," Palmer said.

"You understand, I didn't want to give her the hex. But she threatened to tell my wife about my past, and when I said I had no secrets, she threatened to curse my wife. I had to do what she wanted."

"After Inanna left, what did you do?" Palmer asked.

"I poured myself a strong drink and sat here, in front of the fire. My wife can confirm that if necessary."

I held up the folder of hexes. "After she threatened your wife, you just let her go? You've got powerful evil magic here, and I'm surprised you didn't use it."

"I would never," he said.

"Not even to protect your family? No one would blame you if you did," Palmer said.

"Then why even have all this? It's dangerous." I couldn't believe I'd asked him this, he'd already demonstrated he had no respect for the rules and customs of witches.

"My research is purely theoretical. I never intended for it to be used. Just studied and learned from."

That didn't work out for him. "And how did you feel when she took your work and was going to use it? You know her better than most people, did you think she was going to use it for good? It was a hex, for Brigid's sake, could it ever be used for good?"

I took a breath before my temper got away from me. "Maybe you decided to go after her, get the hex back before she could use it."

He put his head in his hands. "I didn't dare," he whispered. "I stayed home and drank, like a coward." His hands began to shake. "In fact, I could use a nip to steady my nerves."

Palmer looked at me and shook his head. Clive wasn't our murderer. "Thank you for your time. We'll let you get back to your day."

Clive was already pouring himself a shot of clear liquid. "Yes, fine. You can see your way out."

Chapter 13

Palmer dropped me at the apothecary, where I was determined to get in a full day's work. I unlocked the door, prepared to open the shop myself for the first time in what seemed like forever.

After putting my coat and bag away in the office, I lit Trina's candle. "Sorry I haven't been able to chat with you for a while. Life's been busy, mostly in a good way." I sat on the stool behind the counter and stared into the candle. "I've been spending more time with Palmer, and I really like him. He invited all of us to his house for Christmas, and it was amazing. He made so much food for us, and we all had presents under the tree too. I know I'm young, but I think he may be my person. He definitely cares about me even though I'm not a normal person and, honestly, I think he's falling in love with me."

The candle seemed to burn brighter for a moment, but I'm sure that was just my imagination.

"The shop is doing great. I think the best thing I ever did was hire Mackenzie. She's so much better at keeping the shop immaculately clean, and she's really taken to the customers.

They like her as well. I don't know what I'll do if she ever decides to leave."

I stood up and started walking around the shop, looking for anything to clean, tidy, or arrange. Soon, I'd have to put away the New Year's display and create a Valentine's Day one. Lots of floral-scented lotions, some oils, maybe crystals designed to increase your romantic life.

"The family is fine, but the sorority, not so much. We're having issues getting along, and it's because I'm so young and have a familiar. They're not happy that I inherited Jameson when some of them haven't had a familiar for a long time."

I paused as a thought occurred to me. "But Eunice never seemed upset I had Jameson and she didn't. Why not?" I wished I could ask her. I picked up Trina's photo. "I miss you. I feel like I didn't have enough time as your apprentice before I joined the sorority, and I didn't get all the guidance I need."

I set the photo down. Maybe that was what I needed? A new mentor. I'd ask Grandma and Hope what they thought about the idea.

I pulled the hawthorn berry tea from the shelf and started brewing it. The fruity, floral flavor would bring thoughts of spring to the gray, cloudy day.

I poured myself a mug when it finished brewing and got to work in the prep room by putting the candle wax back on the hot plate. "Don't be angry with me, wax. I promise you'll be candles by the end of the day."

Yes, I did talk to my ingredients sometimes. Intention is critical in potion making, and I always thought it couldn't hurt to share your intentions with your materials. I looked at my shelves of ingredients and realized I had plenty of herbs to make a batch of protective ward candles. I'd also make a batch of rose-scented, a batch of unscented pink, and a batch of minor-cold-healing candles. I never questioned where these ideas came from. I assumed it was the goddess guiding me to provide what people needed.

I suspected the rose-scented and pink unscented candles would make it into the Valentine's Day display. The town seemed due for a flu to sweep through too. The protection candles? They were probably for me. At least I had a little warning I'd be in danger soon.

I split the wax into three smaller containers and added red coloring to one. I dipped a wooden tongue depressor into the wax and let it cool, checking it was the right color. Once I got the color right, I stirred the wax for three minutes to make sure the candles would have no streaks of color. As I stirred, I set a small intention that the people who burned these candles would have a good day, full of light and happiness. This was the magical equivalent to wishing someone a nice day. When I finished with my intention, I poured them into the taper molds I'd already put wicks in the last time I made candles. Thank you, past me, for making this a little easier today.

We need to take another look at Chandler House tonight.

Nothing like telepathic demands from your cat to liven up your morning. If you're going to demand things from me, you could at least show up and ask in person.

We'll go after work, they're having a public lecture tonight. Don't be late.

Next up were the rose-scented candles. Scented candles were poured into small glass containers, not turned into tapers. I filled the thirty glass jars and set them aside to cool. For these candles, I added the intention that each person who smelled the rose oil felt loved in whatever way they needed most. This intention was like a gentle magical hug.

I loved my job. In a small way, I was bringing peace to my customers in a time of increasing animosity. Winter was tough on people, and a little extra love and happiness could go a long way.

Finally, the protection candles. These would take a little thought and a lot of intention. Was I really protecting myself, or someone else? And what was I protecting anyone from? I sat in the prep room but no answers came to me. Instead of spending more time there, I decided to move on to other work, hoping the answers would come to me later in the day. "Sorry wax, looks like you're going to cool down again," I said to the last of the unused wax.

I started combining ingredients for hair tonic, harmony bubble bath, and an eczema oil. The oil had to sit for a week before I could strain it and put it on the shelves, while the bubble bath and hair tonic could go out today.

As I was working, there was a knock on the back door. I opened it, with a shield up to protect myself. I wasn't taking the fact I needed protection candles lightly. Alex looked at me quizzically for a moment, and I almost thought he could see my shield before I dropped it.

"Good morning. Nice to see you here today," he said.

I gave him a wide grin. "Nice to see you, too, Alex. Come on in."

I stepped aside and ushered him into my office. "Can I make you some tea? I made hawthorn berry, but I can whip you up anything else you'd like."

"Hawthorn berry sounds good."

He followed me out of my office. "I'm glad you're here this morning, because I'm worried and didn't want to tell Mackenzie."

I poured his tea. "Worried about what?"

"I get this feeling that your shop is being watched. I can't explain it, though. The motion sensing lights don't go on, nothing suspicious is on the video. I just feel it in my gut."

I held up the bottle of honey. "Honey?"

He shook his head. "No, thanks. You probably think I'm just imagining things."

I handed him his mug. "Absolutely not. I've learned to pay attention to my intuition. If you think the shop is being watched, then we need to figure out by who and why."

We walked back into my office and sat. "Is there any pattern? Times or days? Or is it more random?"

He pulled a small notebook out of his jacket pocket and tore a page out of it. "I started keeping track." He handed me the page. "This is what I have so far."

I took the page and read through the dozen dates and times he'd written. "Seems random to me. Do you ever have this feeling during the day, or just at night?"

He took a sip of his tea. "I'm only here at night. But I don't have the same feeling when I'm anywhere else in town during the day."

"I think it's time to formalize our arrangement. I'd like to put you on my payroll as security consultant and pay you a salary."

He looked surprised. "Oh, no. I can't take your money."

"You wouldn't be taking it, you'd be earning it. I'd like you to spend more time during the day around the shop. If you can locate where this feeling is coming from, we might be able to confront it, have it move on." I laughed. "Now you probably think I'm the one making a mountain out of a molehill. Would you be willing to do this for a trial of two weeks?"

He rubbed at the graying stubble on his chin. "I think I can manage that. But minimum wage. I can't take all your money."

I scowled. "Let me ask my accountant what I can afford. I'm certain it will be more than minimum wage. Can you start today?"

He nodded. "I'll stay close to the building and see if I feel anything."

"Let me order you lunch too. It's the least I can do, if you're not going to let me pay you well."

He leaned back in his chair and took a sip of tea. "Do you know anywhere I can get a good homestyle lasagna?"

"I can do you one better than that. There's lasagna in the fridge at Proctor House. I'll ask my mother to bring some over."

"Oh no, I can't . . . it doesn't seem fair to make your mother run around for me. Any restaurant will do."

"I tell you what. I'll call the house and if anyone is coming this way, they can drop some off. If not, I'll order some from The Rosa."

He stood. "I'll just get to work then. It will be helpful if you let me know when you're leaving the building, in case we see a pattern there."

"Alex, thank you. I appreciate you looking out for me."

He nodded and left.

CHIVE RIGHT IN

I leaned back and drank my tea. Why was he looking after me so well? Was it because I let him sleep in a safe place every night? Maybe because I took his warnings seriously. He certainly wasn't in it for the money. New Hampshire's minimum wage was atrociously low.

The door chimes rang, and Mackenzie called my name.

"I'm in the office."

She walked in, hung her coat up, and handed me a coffee and éclair. "I had the feeling you were going to be in today."

Chapter 14

I didn't leave the shop until six that night. I loved leaving my worries at the door and focusing on my customers. Lunch had been a bit weird, though. My mother stopped by and brought two containers of lasagna, already warmed up, but I couldn't find Alex anywhere.

"I'm not sure you should have hired a man who lives on the street to provide security for you. In fact, I'm not sure why you aren't taking care of it yourself. You have all the skills you need."

I frowned. "I do, but I don't want to be here all night hoping to find a prowler. I'd rather have Alex do it."

"Can you even hire him? I mean, does he have the right documentation? Tell me you're not putting your business at risk by paying him under the table."

Now that was something I'd forgotten to consider. Did I want to tell my mother that? No way. "I'm sure it will all work out in the end."

She opened the front door and turned back to me. "Bring the containers back the next time you come to the house, please."

"I will."

Two minutes later, Alex came walking in through the back door.

"I was looking for you. My mother brought us lunch. You should eat it before it gets cold."

He took the container and thanked me. "My wife used to bring me lunch at work. I miss those days."

Did I see his eyes tearing up at the thought of his wife?

"I'll eat this out back. Thank you."

Before I could offer him a seat in the warm office, he was gone. He might not want me to see him tearing up over lasagna, so I said nothing. What was it about him that made me want to reach out and take care of him?

When I went out to tell him I was leaving for the night, Alex told me he hadn't felt anyone snooping around.

"Better luck tonight, and maybe tomorrow," I said. I would have liked to stay and chat with him about his life, but Jameson and I had a date to snoop around Chandler House. On Thursday nights, it was open late to the public and often had historical presentations. Jameson said it would be easiest for us to sneak in with so many other people.

He brought me along as he teleported to Manchester. It tired him, but he didn't want to waste the forty-five minutes driving. We appeared in an alley five blocks from our destination. "Put your glamour on now," he instructed.

I chose to look like a woman in her mid-sixties. Gray hair, liver spots, and a mole on my cheek. Jameson, in a surprising turn, chose to be my cane. I walked the five blocks, perfecting my limp and cane usage. "This doesn't hurt, does it?" I asked as I started walking. "I'm not slamming your head on the ground, am I?"

He answered me telepathically. *It would if I'd put my head at the bottom of the cane. You're putting the equivalent of my feet on the ground. And maybe you shouldn't look like you're talking to yourself.*

Oh, right. Sorry about that.

As I got closer to the house, I pulled a flyer I'd printed from their website announcing the evening's talk, "Cotton, Clothing, and Controversy." I had no idea what the talk was about, but I'd caught Grandma printing flyers from the internet, so I thought it would be good cover for me.

I stopped in front of the house and eyed the eight stairs I had to climb to get in. I sighed as a man walked past me.

"Can I assist you?" he asked.

I looked up at him. He was young, in his mid-twenties. His blond hair peeked out from under his knit hat. I wasn't sure what to say, but Jameson came to my rescue.

He's too young to care about the history of cotton. He's probably with the fraternity. Get him to help you up the stairs.

"Could you help me up the stairs? I'm afraid of slipping on ice."

He smiled at me and held out his arm. "Of course."

I took his arm and he walked at my slower pace up the stairs. I leaned on him and he took my weight easily.

"Are you here for the talk?" he asked.

"I am. It seems the older I get, the more interested I am in looking back to history, rather than forward to the future."

He patted my hand. "You? Old? You're in the prime of your life and don't you let anyone tell you otherwise."

My heart fluttered. Yes, Palmer was never very far from my mind, but a man who treats an older woman well can't be all that bad, can he?

Get your head back in the game.

Bats! I'd forgotten Jameson could read my mind. *Quit that.*

He scoffed. *I didn't mean to. Anyone with telepathic ability just heard you, an old lady, thinking about what a nice young man he is.*

At least I'm in character, right?

Jameson didn't dignify that with an answer.

We reached the top of the stairs and I released his arm. "Thank you very much, young man. What is your name?"

"My name is Kyle, and it was my pleasure. Are you meeting friends tonight?"

"No, I'm afraid not. My best friend, Carol, doesn't like to go out after dark in the winter."

Kyle smiled at me. "Her loss is my gain, then. Would you care to sit with me during the lecture?"

No, I absolutely did not want to sit with him. I wanted to sneak out when no one was looking, but how do you say no to a question like that? "I'd love to. You do your family proud, looking after me."

He held the door open for me. "You remind me of my grandmother, and I like to think that if she were out alone, someone would look after her too. And what should I call you?"

"Oh, silly me," I chuckled. I tried to sound like Grandma, but her chuckle is a little frightening. "I'm—" and I realized I had no name picked out.

Samantha Yeager.

Jameson to the rescue! "I'm Samantha Yeager."

"Follow me, Mrs. Yeager. I come to a lot of these talks and I know how to get the best seats."

We walked into the large lecture room and Kyle spoke to one of the museum employees.

The hall was gorgeous. Each row had ten navy-blue velvet-covered chairs, split in half by a central aisle. The stage mimicked an opera house with heavy curtains and gilt filigree around the walls.

"If you'd like to follow me," the black-clad usher said. He brought us to the front of the room and lifted a worn velvet rope so we could sit.

The usher replaced the velvet rope. Great. Was I trapped here until the talk was over?

"What is your interest in cotton?" I asked Kyle.

"I'm not as interested in cotton as I am in the past. I think I've always been more interested in the past than in the future. I'm a sophomore history major, so these kinds of lectures are fun for me."

I nodded as though I knew how he felt. "Do you have a time period you're most interested in?"

"I'm partial to seventeenth-century America. I'm fascinated by the giant leap of faith the first European colonists made to get in a boat with their families, everything they owned, and set sail for a land they'd never seen before and quite honestly, had very little proof it existed."

"That certainly seems brave. I imagine they felt like they had God on their side, and nothing could go wrong."

He turned to face me, pleased he had someone to talk about his studies with. "We certainly see that in the primary documents of the time. Even when things started to go wrong—not enough food, paranoia, everything that happened before ships began regularly traveling to and from Europe—almost everyone held to their faith."

"It's a comfort for those who believe, I'm sure."

The usher cleared his throat to get our attention. "Excuse me, Mr. Parris. There's a gentleman in the lobby who would like to see you."

That seemed strange. He was just a student, not anyone of particular importance.

Light dawns on marble head, Jameson said sarcastically.

Cauldrons and curses! He's one of the fraternity.

Most likely. Don't look back, but angle me out into the aisle a bit so I can see.

I did as he asked. Parris is speaking to a man, but I can't see who it is. Now is a good time to leave, before he gets back.

I stood up slowly and took my cane. I quickly unhooked the velvet rope and walked to the door at the side of the stage. "Excuse me, young man," I said to a different usher, "is there a ladies' room I could use before the lecture begins?"

"Of course, ma'am." He opened his door for me. "Three doors down on the left. You'll have to come back in through the other door, though. This one is locked from the outside."

I patted his arm in a way I thought sweet, kind little old ladies would. Not that I had any role models in that arena. "Thank you."

I played up my limp as I slowly walked to the ladies' room. Nothing to see here, just an old woman with a pesky bladder.

Once out of sight from everyone else, Jameson changed his glamour to someone who looked almost identical to Kyle.

From a distance he'd pass but, close up, people would realize they were mistaken. "What do I change to?" I asked.

"An usher. We'll use these disguises to get closer to the top floor, then we'll go back to my favorite spy, the spider."

I cast my glamour, giving myself a forgettable face and the black uniform. "Let's go."

We climbed the stairs to the second-floor exhibits without anyone noticing. I followed Jameson to a door marked Emergency Exit. He cast a quick silencing spell on the alarm and pushed the door open. "The other stairs going to the third floor are guarded," he explained.

When we reached the third floor landing, he changed form to a spider. I followed suit, but it didn't feel right. I looked around myself and realized I was a human-sized spider. *A little help here?*

You didn't practice this?

No time. What do I do?

Go back to normal. Shrink first, then turn into a spider.

Shrink first. How do I do that?

The miniaturization spell, Jameson reminded me.

I took a deep breath and allowed my glamour to fall away. I didn't dare look like myself for any longer than necessary here. I cast the miniaturization spell on myself and watched as the walls seemed to rise up around me. Once the wave of vertigo passed, I cast a spider glamour over myself.

Much better. We'll make a half-decent witch out of you yet.

Yeah, well, I don't see you taking anyone else with you on a recon mission. I can't be all that bad.

He scurried under the door and I followed. We remained there for a minute, getting our bearings and deciding what to do next. The room was empty, but we could hear men speaking in the next room.

We're going to sprint around the room. Stick to the baseboards in case someone comes in. If you get crushed as a spider, you'll die just as easily as you would if you were crushed by an elephant.

I didn't like the sound of that. It was a lot easier to be killed as a spider than a human. *Right. I'll follow you.*

He took off at a run. I kept up with him once I stopped looking at my eight legs. Each leg was moving, even though I felt like I was running on two legs and pumping my arms. I'd have to practice this more to get over the disorientation of having a radically different body shape.

We made it to the door on the other side of the room, out of breath but unseen. No one was speaking in the next room. Had we missed the conversation?

Wait here.

I waited, desperately trying to catch my breath and not look like I was completely out of shape. Witches can lead a comfortable life, creating spells and potions, never needing to run anywhere. Investigators, however, needed to run. The holidays were over and so were my excuses for not exercising.

"I need an update on the California situation," a man said.

Jameson came back around the corner. *That was Jake Forster. He's in there with your friend Kyle.*

There was no denying it now. Kyle was a fraternity member. I guess you really couldn't judge a book by its cover.

"We're doing our best to take advantage of the destabilization," Kyle said.

"Doing your best? You should be out there going after every single sorority member. They've got no leader, and ninety percent of them would have killed the one they had if she hadn't bound them with a loyalty spell. Anyone you can't turn in the next day needs to be taken out. Is that understood?"

"Yes, boss. We've turned fifteen already."

Forster's voice lowered. "Not nearly enough. We can take the state if we move quickly."

"I'll leave now," Kyle said.

Jameson risked another look around the corner. *Forster is alone now. We should go.*

I agreed. I wanted to warn Winter and Raven their entire coven was in danger.

But what about your sister?

The two of us aren't strong enough. We need to come back with more people.

I'm sorry. I promise we'll save her.

He ran back along the wall to the door that led to the emergency stairs. Once we were on the stairs, he changed his glamour to a human form. I turned myself into an usher.

"There's an exit on the first floor. We'll take that and teleport as soon as we get outside."

I nodded. We quietly crept down the two flights of stairs to the fire exit. Jameson silenced the alarm and pushed the door open. He took my hand, pulled me out of the building, and immediately teleported back to Proctor House.

Chapter 15

We appeared in the kitchen of Proctor House. We both dropped our glamours immediately, so no one would think the house was under attack.

"I need to sleep," Jameson said. "Carting you around was harder than I thought it would be."

I scratched between his ears. "Take my bed."

He slowly walked out of the kitchen, and I realized he must be exhausted if he didn't even demand food before bed. I needed to warn Winter and Raven about the fraternity's plan for California, but I couldn't teleport. I pulled out my phone and called Hope.

"Hi, Hope, it's Isabella."

"Is something wrong?" she asked.

"Yes. The fraternity is planning to take over the California coven and we need to warn them."

"What are you talking about?"

"Jameson and I were at Chandler House tonight, and we heard them talking about taking over the California sorority, or killing all its members. I need to warn them."

"I'll take care of it. This needs a face-to-face meeting."

My heart sank. "No, don't go. The fraternity is already there, and there's no reason they wouldn't go after you too."

She chuckled. "I should be fine for the ten minutes I'm there."

I still didn't like her going into danger. "Call me when you get back so I don't worry, okay?"

"Will do," she said.

I'd planned to go back to my apartment for the night but, with the fraternity on the move and actively planning to kill witches, I decided not to. I felt safer at Proctor House, surrounded by family.

Hope didn't call, but she texted me about an hour after I called her, letting me know she was back home and safe. Over breakfast, Palmer called.

"I need you to come down to the station, right away."

I was still in my pajamas and hadn't taken a shower yet. "Okay. Let me get dressed and finish my breakfast."

"You might want to skip breakfast," he said.

Unease prowled in my stomach. "What happened?"

"We've got a dead patrolman, and the circumstances look like something you can help me with."

I grabbed a piece of toast and stood. "I'll be there as soon as I can." I rushed upstairs, trying to finish eating, get dressed, and pull my hair back all at once. I grabbed the car keys from the hook in the kitchen and kissed Aunt Nadia. "Tell Thea and Delia it was an emergency, and I'm sorry."

I drove quickly but safely to the station. Palmer was waiting for me at the door. He looked at my feet. "Thanks for rushing, but you could have put real shoes on."

I looked down and saw I was still in my slippers. No one could see my feet but Palmer, so I wiggled a finger at them and cast a tiny glamour. "Better?"

"Maybe? Are those real boots or do they just look like boots?"

"It's just a glamour, so I'm still wearing my slippers. But I also cast the warming spell so my toes won't get cold."

"Good."

"What happened that I had to come here right away and now you're not letting me into the building?"

He stood aside and let me in. "Oh, sorry. Let's talk in the conference room."

That couldn't be good. What kind of magic happened that he couldn't rephrase it to make the events sound normal to anyone who was listening to us talk?

I took a seat at the table. "What could possibly be so bad?"

"We found some anomalous license plates in the area of the library when we thought Inanna's body was dumped. I asked a new officer—Josh Sullivan—to check on them." He rubbed his face with his hand. "He was only supposed to do a records check. But he found one car from Manchester that he followed up on in person."

I was pretty sure I knew where this was going. "Chandler House?"

Palmer nodded.

"What makes you think you need me for this?"

Palmer sat next to me. "His body appeared out back. Out of the blue. I watched the video. He wasn't there, then he was."

"Teleportation," I said.

His eyes widened. "That's a thing you can do?"

I shook my head. "Not yet. But witches in general, yes."

"How did you know it was Chandler House?" he asked.

"It's the New Hampshire headquarters for the fraternity. Jameson and I were there last night, but we didn't see any police there."

"There was a public lecture, he went to see it. I guess he thought he'd be able to investigate while everyone else was in the lecture hall."

"So what do you want me to do?" I asked. "I can look at the video, but I doubt I'll pick up more than you did."

"I need your help. Your sorority's help. I can't send more of my people in, they're defenseless against magic. Sullivan deserves justice, but the police are powerless to get it for him."

I put my hand on his. "Of course we'll help. Do you know who killed him?"

He looked away from me. "No. We've got nothing. I'm happy to drag everyone from the fraternity down here and question them. I've had it with this group. How many other murders have they gotten away with?"

I shrugged. "I don't know."

"It's not enough to keep arresting them one at a time. As an organized group there are federal statutes—the RICO Act, or maybe we can get them for tax evasion. I don't care. I'll take jaywalking if I can get them off the streets and build a stronger case against them."

He was shaking with rage at this point.

"You need to calm down. Let's think this through and come up with a plan that doesn't have the fraternity murdering your entire department, okay?"

He stood and looked out the door. "The longer we wait, the more people they're going to kill. It's only a matter of time before they come after you."

"You agree we can't have any other police involved, right?"

He turned to me. "We have to tell the chief. But no one else."

I didn't like the idea of involving any more non-witches than necessary. "I suppose we have to, don't we?"

Palmer nodded.

"You bring him up to speed and I'll get everyone else together. We'll have a plan by nightfall, and we can implement it tonight."

He grabbed my arm. "Oh no. You're not leaving my sight until this is over."

Of all the people involved, he was the least capable of protecting me. But I couldn't tell him that. "Let's be quick about it then."

I closed the chief's door and put up a silencing spell around the three of us. The chief dropped the file he was reading. "Looks grim. Tell me all about it."

We sat and Palmer filled him in. "Sullivan's body was dumped out back."

The chief looked confused. "Wasn't he doing records checks for you?"

Palmer nodded. "He found something and decided to investigate last night. Didn't tell anyone, just left me a note." He took a deep breath. "He's at the morgue now."

The chief frowned. "He should have known better than that. How did he die?"

"It was magic. If you look at the video, one second the alley is empty, then Sullivan's body blinks into existence. I had Dr. Hathaway pick him up."

Chief Dobbins looked at me. "Your family is wrapped up in this, isn't it?"

I sighed. "Yes. And the sorority. We're going to take care of it tonight, but we need you to keep everyone away. The fraternity is much bolder, and stronger now. They won't hesitate to kill police and, if I'm right and they killed Inanna, they're strong enough to take out some of our best if she's alone." I looked out at the police in the large open office. "Your people don't stand a chance."

He thought for a moment. "What do you need me to do?"

"Keep everyone away from Chandler House, in Manchester, tonight," Palmer said.

"That's not going to be easy. I can't just call up Chief Huizinga and tell him what to do in his city," the chief said. "He'll want his people involved."

"We can't let that happen," I said. "His people could be slaughtered."

Palmer looked at me. "Can't you just"—he wiggled his fingers—"make it look like nothing was going on at the house?"

I couldn't help but laugh and wiggle my fingers back at him. "Yes. We could put up a spell around the house to keep everyone else from seeing what was going on."

"Good. Then I'm coming with you."

I started to protest, but he held up his hand to stop me. "I've spent too long trying to pretend magic doesn't exist. Until now, there weren't any consequences to me keeping my head in the sand. I'm not losing more good people because I don't want deal with reality."

I wasn't sure how my family would react to his change of heart. "Aunt Lily might—"

"I'll talk to her and we'll work it out."

"You'll need to talk to Grandma too. She's not your biggest fan."

He grimaced. "She might take more time to come around, but she's not a fool and will see that the plan will call for me to deal with its more mundane aspects."

I hoped he was right. Palmer would have a hard time explaining how the chief got turned into a toad.

Chapter 16

On the drive to Proctor House, I contacted Grandma and Hope, telling them to gather everyone at the house. It was time to take the fraternity down.

We met in the large dining room. Seven witches from the sorority, my six other family members, Palmer, Dobbins, and Jameson. Sixteen of us to invade and stop the fraternity. We were going to need a good plan.

Hope started us off by introducing Palmer and the chief to everyone. "They have no magic, and we need to protect them at all costs."

"All costs? I'm not sure I'm willing to risk my life for one of them," Anna said. "In the end, I can do more good than both of them put together."

Aunt Lily flushed with anger. "You won't need to. I'll protect Ray."

"And I'll protect Palmer," I said. There was no way I'd put his safety into the hands of a witch who didn't care if he lived or died.

Hope slowly looked around the room. "We will all protect each other. Is that clear? These men put their lives in danger every time it is required of them, and I'd better not hear anyone discussing how one life is more valuable than another ever again."

By the time she finished, her voice was just below a yell. I'd never seen her so angry before.

"We are done. Done with these foolish ideas about who deserves to be where. Who deserves a familiar and who doesn't. We are a team and by the goddess we will start acting like one. If you're not willing to, you can give me your amulet and show yourself out."

Had Hope really just said she'd accept any resignation from the sorority? I held my breath, wondering if anyone would take her up on it.

After a minute of complete stillness, Hope continued. "Good. Now that we've got that out of the way, let's get to work. Detective Palmer, how do you think we should approach this?"

Palmer stood and walked to the head of the table. "Thank you, Hope. I may not have all the details about magic right, so feel free to chime in when I get something wrong." He looked around the kitchen. "Do we have something to write on in here?"

We didn't. "What do you need to write?" I asked.

"If we all could see what I was talking about, there would be less opportunity for confusion once we got to the house. But we can make do without a diagram."

I projected an image of Chandler House in the center of the table. "Will this work?"

He grinned at me. "Perfect. I see this operation going down in several steps. First, we make it so no one sees us driving up to the property. I think—"

"Hold on there, big guy," Christina interrupted. "Why would we drive? Why not teleport? It would be easier and less conspicuous than if a bunch of cars suddenly parked near the house."

"Oh, thank you. I didn't know that was an option. The chief and I will drive, and you will all meet us there."

"Aunt Lily and I will go with you," I said. Everyone knew I couldn't teleport yet, but I needed to stay with Palmer anyway. "Aunt Nadia and mom can bring Thea and Delia along with them."

"Good. We'll meet two blocks east of the property. At that time, someone needs to make sure no one follows us to the house."

"Simple cloaking spell," Grandma said. "I'll take care of that."

"And when we get to the house, we need to make it look like nothing is happening. We don't want neighbors calling about a disturbance, because we're keeping the Manchester police out of it."

"I can take care of that. I won't be as useful in capturing fraternity members, though. If I split my focus too much, I'll lose the illusion over the house," Claire said.

"Noted," Palmer said. He looked at the house for a moment. "It looks like there are three entrances. We'll have to cover each of them, leaving one person behind to catch anyone who tries to escape."

I added images of us, some at each door, making sure I was with Palmer and the chief was with Aunt Lily.

"Cool," Palmer said. "The second phase is the initial incursion into the house. We don't want to set off any alarms—physical or magical. Can someone take care of that?"

"One witch at each door will need to take care of that," Hope said.

I added an image of an alarm over the head of one witch at each door.

Helen frowned. "Who said she gets to assign tasks? What if I don't want to disable the alarms?"

Hope scowled at her. "Let's go with the assignments for now, and you can switch jobs within your group later."

Helen leaned back in her chair, but didn't say anything else.

"Once we're sure we're all in, the third phase is to spread out and arrest anyone we find."

I raised my hand. "Uh . . . most of us can't do that."

He winked at me. "But if you look like police, they'll never know the difference."

"And do you expect these people to just stop fighting when they hear the words 'you're under arrest'?" Sasha asked. "Because I can tell you for certain they'll laugh in our faces, just before they kill us."

"Excellent question, Sasha. Here I need to rely on your expertise. We want to somehow sneak up on each person and teleport them to the holding cells in Portsmouth. And we can't let the rest of the station see how they get there."

"Not asking for much, are you?" Thea said.

"Are you telling me that thirteen witches can't manage this if they work together?" Palmer asked.

"It would be a lot easier if we teleported in and out quickly, grabbing the closest person we saw," Delia said.

I shook my head. "We can't. The building is locked down tight. No one can teleport in or out, not even fraternity members."

My mother glared at me. "How do you know that, Isabella?"

I looked to Jameson, who flicked his tail but said nothing, not even to me.

"Jameson and I were there last night."

Palmer saw anger cross my mother's face and started talking quickly. "Who else has an idea?"

"We've got to get each person out of the building first? That's going to be conspicuous. Once we start, anyone not caught immediately will escape," the chief said.

"It would be easier if we set the building on fire, then grabbed them as they ran out," Grandma said.

"You want to set fire to a historical landmark?" Delia asked.

"Can we contain the fire to just the one building?" the chief asked.

"How about a fire illusion?" Aunt Nadia countered.

That might not work. The illusion may fall apart once it entered the house. "How about we pump smoke through the building, and they think there's a fire when it's real smoke, no illusion?" I asked.

"I like it. This keeps everyone out of the house, which keeps us all safer," Palmer said. "Can you make enough smoke to fill the house quickly?"

"Hope and I can. We've done it before," Grandma chuckled.

Hope laughed. "Let's not talk about that now, though."

I had to ask to hear the story later, but I could already imagine two much younger women getting into trouble over this.

"Okay. Let's talk about this idea for a minute. We still station ourselves outside the building, at the doors, and the invisibility spell is still working. Everyone who can will generate smoke and force it into the building. The windows will all be closed. How will you get it in there?"

The chief leaned forward. "Old houses are far from airtight. I think they'll be able to find cracks, areas around the windows, and even chimneys to force the smoke into the building."

"Our house is old and, even though we've updated the windows, it's still drafty," Grandma said. "Hope, let's go outside and try."

The two women left the room and three minutes later, smoke started flowing into the house from the windows, the fireplace, and even the corners of the room.

"Okay Grandma," I called out as I opened the window. "It's working well."

I let the smoke dissipate until Hope and Grandma came back inside. "That worked great."

"Okay. On to phase—I don't know what phase, since we changed everything around. Anyway, we get there, we smoke them out, then you teleport them back to Portsmouth." Palmer looked to the chief. "But where?"

"Definitely inside the station, so they can't escape," Hope said.

"Interrogation rooms?" I asked.

"That could work," the chief said. "I'll have to stay there to organize booking the fraternity members."

"Someone will have to be there to escort us out of the building so we can come back though. I don't want anyone mistaking me for a criminal," Claire said.

"And someone will have to be there to make sure no one is using the room, too," I said.

We all looked at the chief. He was the right person for the job. "I don't want to stay behind, but I'm not going to be any good to you in Manchester, and it's a waste to have Lily focus on keeping me safe because I can't take care of myself in the moment."

"If that's the case, do we need him?" Sasha asked, looking at Palmer.

He looked like someone took the wind out of his sails. "I don't imagine a gun is much use when fighting magic, is it?"

I shook my head. "No. But you can work with the chief to get everyone into the cells. The fewer people who see what's going on, the better. We're all Team Sorority here, and everyone has an important part to play."

"It goes against my training to stay behind and let other people take on the danger," he said.

Hope clapped her hands. "Excellent. It sounds like we have a plan. Those witches who can't teleport will, along with Jameson, rescue his sister Jennifer. You start once the building is cleared. While you're waiting, you can immobilize anyone who looks like they're going to escape."

Palmer sat back down in his chair and Hope resumed her place at the head of the table. "Ladies, this will take cooperation and focus. We have a real chance to bring down part of the fraternity tonight. Let's not waste it on petty rivalries."

Around the table, every witch nodded solemnly.

Hope looked at her watch. "It's noon right now. Take the next few hours to prepare. We'll meet two blocks east of Chandler House at four o'clock."

Palmer stayed behind and, when the sorority left, he asked to speak to me in private. My family left us alone in the large dining room, but I wasn't sure no one would eavesdrop, so I suggested we go outside.

Once we were in the backyard, he took my hand. "I don't think I can do this."

I took a deep breath of the cold January air. "What do you mean?"

"Play a supporting role while you put yourself in danger."

I knew this moment would come sooner or later, if I kept working cases with him. "I know it's difficult. Because I do it all the time. You confront murderers while I hang back. That is, if I am even there. You have nothing but a gun to protect yourself."

"Nothing but a gun? It's done fine so far."

I shook my head. "Look at it from my perspective. You've got bullets. I've got binding spells, tripping spells, confusion spells, more potions than I could name, and a family full of witches to back me up when I run out of magic to use myself. The police only have guns. In the face of magic, you're almost defenseless."

I knew he wouldn't like hearing how weak he was compared to even a young witch but, if our relationship was going to survive, he needed to know I could take care of myself.

"It grates against all my training," he said with frustration.

"Your job is to protect and serve. Maybe tonight you serve more than protect. We take the fraternity off the streets and you keep them off."

"If anything happens to you . . ."

"You'll be part of a long line of people looking for retribution. But nothing's going to happen to me."

"Inanna probably thought the same thing," he said.

She probably did. "But I'm not alone. I've got twelve other witches and my familiar with me."

"And there's nothing I can do to keep you home tonight, is there?"

I frowned at him. "Absolutely not. That's not even an okay question to ask me. You need to make your peace with the fact that I am"—inspiration hit me—"a magical law enforcement agent. The sorority enforces our laws just like you enforce yours."

He didn't say anything to that, but I could tell he was thinking and trying to reconcile the conflicting thoughts in his head.

"Go back to work, or go home, and think about this for a while. If you can't reconcile yourself to the way I lead my life, the danger my position in the sorority puts me in, then we may not have a future together."

I didn't like saying it, but the time had come. I would be heartbroken if he couldn't accept the situation, but I'd rather know now than later, after I'd fallen more in love with him.

Chapter 17

Aunt Lily called the chief at a quarter of four. He assured her he and Palmer were ready.

"How many people are you expecting?" he asked.

"Honestly, Ray, I'm not sure. Jameson said there are usually a dozen fraternity members there but, some nights, the number can be much higher."

"I'll make sure we've got enough space for them all. And, Lily, take care of yourself. I'd hate to see you get hurt."

"I will. You too. Their first instinct will be to use magic to escape, but don't forget they can break out just as easily with force."

Aunt Lily hung up the phone and turned to us. "They're all set. Shall we go?"

"Just a minute." I created a life-sized image of Kyle and Forster. "We particularly want to catch these two men. On the left is a man named Kyle, and on the right is Jake Forster."

Thea, Delia, and I teleported with our mothers. Jameson needed a rest from, as he said, carrying my large self around. I didn't think I was particularly large, but I suppose compared to his ten or so pounds, I was huge.

There was a diner on the corner we were to meet at. "Let's go inside and get out of the sleet," I suggested.

"Don't mind me, I'll just stay out here in the cold," Jameson said.

"I've seen your human glamour. You could absolutely join us if you wanted to, so stop complaining."

He thought about it for a moment, but decided to stay outside. "I'll keep watch until it's time to go."

We took up most of the counter and each ordered coffee. Grandma ordered a slice of pecan pie too. "What? I don't want to head out hungry," she said when I looked at her pie.

I was too nervous to eat. Maybe by the time I was her age I'd have seen enough that pecan pie sounded good right before a mass arrest and hostage rescue.

The rest of the sorority arrived minutes later and took up a large table. The one waitress on duty rushed around, getting coffee and desserts for them.

"We've taken care of the first step," Hope told us on her way to the ladies' room.

That was good. No one would see what we were up to, or even see us circling the building, as we prepared to smoke everyone out. I had a moment of panic. *Jameson, what if your sister breathes too much smoke?*

She's in the basement. As long as you keep the smoke away from her, she'll be fine. Tell everyone else, would you?

Will do.

At five minutes before four, we all stood to leave. I was sure our waitress was confused, but we'd probably never see her again. On the walk, I told everyone to keep the smoke away from the basement.

CHIVE RIGHT IN

One block away from Chandler House, we took turns pulling on an invisibility spell that we would drop only once we reached our assigned door. I called Palmer to tell him we would be in position in two minutes, then stepped inside the invisibility spell that surrounded the house.

At four on the dot, we all began creating smoke and funneling it into the house. The fraternity must not have taken good care of the building, because the smoke found its way inside quickly. After a minute, I heard a fire alarm and then my door crashed open.

Grandma grabbed the first person out the door and vanished with him. Hope grabbed the next person out, then Anna and my mother. Grandma hadn't returned yet, so I prepared my ensnaring spell. An older woman rushed out of the building, and I hesitated. Was she a museum patron? I knew she wasn't as she vanished before my eyes.

One got away, I told everyone on Team Sorority.

Grandma returned and took away the next person who left the building. Hope took the last person to exit our door. After five more minutes, no one had left. *I think that's everyone. Let's sweep the house.* We left a guard at each door—Grandma at mine, because I knew she'd never hesitate like I did—and we swept each floor, starting with the first.

Everyone was out of the building. Jameson, go get your sister. I'll meet you there.

I met him in the basement, Thea and Delia right behind me. We looked at the magic trapping Jennifer, and I called to Grandma and the aunts for help releasing the bindings. They were intricately knotted together, and I didn't know how to remove one without triggering another.

Grandma was the first downstairs. "Can we force all spells in and on the house to stop?" I asked.

"No chance. There's too much going on here. I'm afraid that we'll hit a trap."

The aunts arrived and started looking at the different spells. "Very tricky," my mother said.

If you don't get the order right, you'll set off a lightning bolt spell. It only missed me because I'm not human-sized, Jameson said.

"I'd start with this one," Aunt Lily said as she pointed to an entrapment circle chalked on the floor, too far away for Jennifer to reach it.

"Hold on a moment, let me see."

"Jennifer, do you know how all these are put together? Can you help us figure out how to get you out safely?" I asked.

She began meowing, and Jameson answered her. When she was done, he said, "They put the entrapment circle in last, so she thinks starting with it is best. She was under a spell and doesn't remember anything they did before it though."

Grandma nodded. "Go ahead, Lily, break the circle."

Aunt Lily rubbed the chalk with her foot until the circle broke. As it did, one of the spells holding Jennifer began to tighten.

"Bats! We've got to remove that one next. Girls, focus on it and imagine it loosening while I work on it."

I wasn't sure which girls Grandma was referring to, but I did as she said. The spell was strong, and it wasn't until the aunts, my cousins, and I were all trying to loosen it that it stopped constricting. Grandma tried one spell that had no effect.

"Hold on, I think I've got it," Grandma said. She rapidly cast another spell, and the constricting spell vanished.

Jennifer stood up and shook, almost like a wet dog, and three other spells vanished.

"One more spell and she'll be free," Grandma said. "Lily, use your shearing spell on it."

Aunt Lily cast her shearing spell, and we all felt the last spell crack, then fade away. Jameson bounded forward and the two cats ran outside without a word. I didn't blame them. There would be plenty of time to talk once we were safe at home.

"All right, ladies, it's time to go," Hope said. "We'll meet back at Proctor House."

My mother grasped my hand and we all teleported back to Proctor House. Jules and Jessamin were sitting next to Jennifer, their mother, meowing and rubbing against her.

Aunt Nadia began poaching salmon for the cats, and I poured bowls of milk for each of them. Tonight was a night to celebrate.

I called Palmer to let him know we were done.

"Did you get the cat too?" he asked.

"We did. It was tricky, but she's home with us now."

"I'm going to start interrogating now. Do you want to join me? Or maybe someone else from the sorority?" he asked.

"I'll do it. I'll be there in a half an hour."

"I'll wait for you then."

Hope dismissed the sorority with her thanks for a job well done. We hadn't captured Forster, but there was no guarantee he would have been there.

"I'm going to help Palmer interrogate the witches we caught. Maybe we'll be able to figure out who got away."

My mother gave me a hug. "Don't beat yourself up over losing one. We made a big dent in their numbers, at least here in New Hampshire, and they'd be wise to think twice about coming back."

Thea tossed me the keys to the car. "We won't need it tonight."

As I drove to the police station, I wondered if Palmer would have an answer for me. Was he ready to treat me like another law enforcement professional? I hoped he would, but I wasn't sure what he'd say. Or if he'd even say anything yet.

Chapter 18

I walked into the police station and there was a buzz of confusion everywhere.

"I just don't know where they came from."

"The chief says they were brought in through the back, but I didn't notice anything."

"Something weird is going on here."

Palmer met me at the reception desk and we went into the observation room for the first interrogation room. "You've got a problem," I said.

He grabbed me in a tight embrace. "We can talk about that in a minute."

He didn't say anything else as he held me tightly. "Hey, I'm fine. Never even the hint of a problem today. They didn't know what hit them."

He released me and looked deeply into my eyes. "I know you can handle yourself. I've never dated another cop before, and this will take a little getting used to, but I'll do my best."

Relief coursed through me. I didn't want to break up with him, but I would have. "You've got a problem with your officers. They know something's happened, and they're not believing whatever story the chief has put out. You need to stop their speculation before it gets out of hand."

"How?"

I shrugged. "Maybe he can tell them it was an FBI operation and he couldn't tell anyone before it was over."

He furrowed his eyebrows at me. "I'm not sure I like how quickly you came up with that lie."

I laughed. "We all get inspired once in a while." I turned to the window. "Who have we got here?"

"Paul Berry. He was the most nervous-looking one down in the holding cells. I figured we'd have an easier time turning him than anyone else."

I nodded. "Okay. I need to know three things. Who killed Inanna, who killed your officer, and where Forster is."

"Can your sorority handle Forster on its own?" he asked.

"Honestly, I don't know. I suspect he's in California, and we may need help from Winter, Raven, and anyone else that hasn't defected from the sorority to catch him."

"Ready to go?" he asked.

I nodded. "One more thing."

He stopped turning the door handle and turned back to me. "Yes?"

"I'm glad I didn't have to break up with you."

"Me too," he said.

We walked into the interrogation room and Berry's eyes widened. "Oh no. I'm not talking in front of her. She's with the enemy, and you've got to get her out of here."

Palmer looked to me, then to him. "What are you talking about?"

Berry motioned for Palmer to come closer. He did, then Berry whispered, "She's a sorority witch. You can't trust them."

I stood still, not letting any emotion cross my face.

"What do you mean? Witches don't exist, man. That's just all made-up Halloween stuff," Palmer said.

Berry shook his head. "No, that's not true. Witches exist. And the bad ones will kill you the second you cross them. I'm telling you, you can't trust her."

Palmer put his hand on Berry's shoulder. "Okay. Let's send her out for coffee and we can talk in private. Does that work for you?"

"I'm not drinking anything she brings me, and you shouldn't either. This one runs a potion shop, and there's no telling what kind of poisons she knows how to make, and what she's willing to use them for."

Palmer turned to me. "Miss Proctor, would you please get me a cup of coffee?"

I had no idea what he was planning to do, but I was sure he had something in mind. "Of course."

I left, but went into the observation room.

"Tell me, why do you think magic exists?" Palmer asked.

Berry realized he'd already said too much and snapped his lips shut.

Palmer sat across the table from the suspect. "It's okay, you can tell me. I've always thought there was a little something off about her. I could just never put my finger on it."

"What do you mean?" Berry asked.

"You know, little stuff that never added up. Like she's never wet when she comes in from the rain. She never has a bad hair day, either."

Berry barked a laugh. "You ever hear of umbrellas? Or wigs?"

Palmer shook his head. "No, man, we can be out together in the rain and she still never gets wet."

Berry leaned back in his chair. "Sloppy work, that. She should know better than to let other people see the effects of her spells."

"You think she can cast spells?"

Berry smiled. "I know she can. The problem is, you never know if she's going to cast them for you or against you."

Palmer laughed. "Nah, I can't believe that. Witches don't exist."

"How do you think I got here, then? How did so many people just show up in your interrogation room?"

Berry was making a convincing case for magic right now, but I still didn't know where Palmer was going with the interrogation.

"The chief said you were brought in by the FBI, through the back door."

Berry shook his head. "Nah, that's not what happened. I was in Manchester, just minding my business at a museum. Suddenly, the whole building is full of smoke and the fire alarm went off. Of course we all left and, the second I was out of the building, some old lady—another witch—grabbed me and teleported me here. I don't even know where I am."

"You're at the Portsmouth police station. The FBI seems to think they have a strong case against you and everyone else they brought in."

For the first time, Berry looked afraid. "Case for what?"

Palmer shook his head. I wished I could see both of them, but I was stuck looking at Berry's face and the back of Palmer's head.

"Can't say just yet. You'll know when we arrest you."

Berry got a sly look. "Wait a minute. I'm not under arrest?"

"Did anyone read you your rights? Offer you your one phone call?"

"No. Nothing. You're the first person I've talked to since I got here."

I rushed back into the room with a random file I picked up off the table. "Here you go, boss. Thought you'd like to see this."

Palmer flipped through the file and set it on the table, face down. "Mr. Berry, there seems to have been an error on our part. You're free to go."

"What about everyone else?" he asked.

"Oh no, they've been properly arrested. You're the only one we got wrong."

Palmer stood up to unlock his handcuffs.

"Of course, you realize the minute you leave, the rest of your friends in the cells will think you told us everything," I said.

The color in his face drained.

"You know as well as I do, it will only take one phone call to Jake Forster. If just one of them calls him, tells him you never came back from your interrogation, your life expectancy will be measured in minutes," I said.

Palmer unlocked Berry's cuffs. Now was the critical moment. Would he rat on his friends to save his life, or would he sacrifice himself for the fraternity?

Berry rubbed his wrists. "Let's say I wanted to get arrested. All I'd have to do is assault either one of you, right?"

Palmer put his hand on Berry's shoulder, pressing him into the chair so he couldn't get up. "That won't be necessary, Mr. Berry. You can confess to a crime. Make it useful to us, or we can't be responsible for what Forster might do to you when we release you."

Berry held his arms out. "Put the cuffs back on. I need to confess."

Palmer didn't take his hand off Berry's shoulder. "Confess to what?"

"I did a dine and dash last week at the Thirsty Moose."

Palmer shook his head. "Not good enough. I'm a detective, and the chief expects me to bring in murder suspects, felons, not weasely little guys who split on a check."

Berry looked desperate. "But I don't do that kind of stuff. I'm in charge of the back office. I pay the bills, book the speakers for the museum. Once in a while I go out and scare tourists."

Palmer took his hand off Berry's shoulder. "You're free to go, Mr. Berry, with the thanks of the Portsmouth police for your assistance."

Berry didn't move. "No, wait. How about if I tell you a crime someone else did? Would that be good enough? I could say I helped, even though they'd never let me in on a big operation."

"I don't know. Tell me all about this supposed crime."

Wow! I know I told Palmer I was his equal but, bats and branches, was he good at getting people to tell him what he wanted to know. I was, too, but I used . . . friendliness, I guess, and he used disbelief and Berry's own fears against him. I liked my method better, but there was no denying Palmer was good.

"There's this guy, Kyle. He's high up in our group. Forster uses him for some of the ugly work that has to get done. Anyway, I heard Kyle reporting back to Forster about a noise in the basement, saying that he found one of the California witches and took care of her."

I froze every muscle on my face and left the room. Once I closed the door, I leaned against the wall. Kyle? That didn't seem right. I knew he wasn't really a history student at a local college, but I didn't think a person who would help an old lady up the stairs would kill a different old lady just days before.

This, I realized, was how your heart got hardened as you got older. I went out to the kitchen for some coffee. The goddess was looking out for me, because Papatonis was making a fresh pot.

"Hi, Miss Proctor. I didn't realize you were here today."

I smiled at him. "I am. Palmer wanted my help with an interrogation."

Papatonis turned from the coffee maker to look at me. "Sure is weird, so many people showing up like that. We didn't even have word that a major operation was going on in town today."

He stopped talking and continued to look at me.

"I can't say anything, but I'm sure you'll all be briefed when the time is right. The chief isn't someone to keep things from his people, is he?"

"I suppose not. It's just weird, you know?"

I nodded and opened the fridge. I pulled out a handful of creamers and set them on the counter. I took sugar packets and put everything in a paper cup. The coffee pot was half full. "How's the family?"

Papatonis smiled and pulled out his phone. "My little sister won gold in a ski meet last weekend." He held up the phone to show me his lock screen. I couldn't make out her features, with the hat, large goggles, and coat zipped up past her chin. But she was wearing a gold medal.

"That's fantastic. You must be so proud."

"I am. I keep telling her she needs to go to college in Colorado so she can get Olympic-level training, and acclimate to breathing so high up. I think she can make it to the games in a couple years."

The coffee maker spit out the last of the hot water, letting us know it was done brewing.

"Can I pour you a cup?" he asked.

"Two. One for me and one for Palmer, please."

He handed me two full cups. I nested one in the cup of creamer and sugar packets.

"You're going to spill. Let me help with that."

I handed him one of the coffees. "Thanks. I hate burning myself with coffee." And I did, even though it used to be a common occurrence when I worked at the Fancy Tart. Surprisingly, I hadn't burned myself at the apothecary.

I opened the door to the interrogation room and brought Palmer his coffee. I took mine from Papatonis and shut the door on him. I knew he was curious, but we couldn't let him hear Palmer's questions.

Palmer had put Berry's handcuffs back on, so I guess he had confessed to enough.

"The murder of the old lady, Inanna Blackwing. Lots of petty theft. There's one more murder I need to know about."

Berry looked at Palmer's coffee, then to me, then back to Palmer. "Okay, I heard about one more, but it wasn't directly from the source, if you know what I mean."

He stared silently as Palmer tore open two sugar packets, emptied them into his coffee, then added creamer.

"Listen, honestly. Don't drink the coffee. You never know what she's put in it. She was out there for a long time."

Palmer looked at me. "Did you put anything in my coffee?"

I shook my head. "No, but I didn't make it. One of the other officers did. I just carried it over here."

He picked up his cup and took a long sip. Berry looked horrified, like he expected Palmer to fall over dead at any second.

"Tell me everything about the last murder."

"There was this guy, he came snooping around one night. Anyone could tell he wasn't there for the lecture, and he kept asking a bunch of weird questions. So Forster had Jimmy take care of him."

"Which one is Jimmy?"

"I didn't see him downstairs. I think he might have gotten away."

Bats. I let a cop killer go. I'd have to get the sorority to help me track him down.

"How do you know he did it?" Palmer asked.

"He asked a bunch of us to get rid of the body."

Palmer shifted in his seat. "Portsmouth Public Library again?"

Berry shook his head. "No. This time, they teleported him to your back door. They thought it would be fun to dump him and run, you know, and get away with it."

Palmer's jaw clenched. "Who dumped him?"

"A couple of the new guys. I don't know their names, but I saw them downstairs."

"Get up," Palmer said. "I'm bringing you back to the cells, and you're going to find out who they are. When you do, you're going to demand your phone call, and then you're going to tell me. Is that clear?"

Berry nodded.

"If you don't get back to me in an hour, I'm going to set you free. You know what happens then."

Papatonis was waiting outside the interrogation room. Palmer thrust Berry at him. "Take him back to the cells."

"Sure thing, boss," Papatonis said.

"You okay?" Palmer asked once Berry had turned the corner.

"Yeah. It got a little rough in there, but you did it." I took a sip of my coffee. "I met Kyle the night Jameson and I did some recon at the museum. I looked like a little old lady, and he helped me up the stairs. He brought me to the front so I could see and hear well. I'm having a hard time reconciling that with the fact he murdered Inanna."

"You may never know why he chose to be kind to you, but it's not wise to assume he'll be kind again."

"Kyle went to California yesterday. Forster told him to take advantage of the instability in their sorority."

Palmer closed his eyes. "We've got the same problem. Police can't bring him in. Can you go to California to get him, or should the local sorority take care of it?"

"I don't know. Probably all of us. I want in on his interrogation—as my old lady self—when we do get him. I want him to know I was watching him, and he had no idea."

Palmer nodded. "You bring him to me, and I'll make sure you're here."

"Good. Now I need to get home and figure out how we're going to catch Kyle and Forster."

He took my hand. "Come back to me in one piece."

"I will." I hoped I was telling the truth.

Chapter 19

The drive home went by in a blur, and I pulled into Proctor House's driveway before I realized it. The family was relaxing in the living room, talking about the raid on Chandler House.

"What happened with the interrogations?" Grandma asked when she saw me enter the room.

I sank into a chaise and put my feet up. "Palmer got one of them, Paul Berry, to turn on the others. A man named Kyle killed Inanna, on Forster's orders. We didn't catch Kyle or Forster tonight, and I think they probably went to California."

"I've got to tell Hope," Grandma said.

"I'll do it, that way I can tell her everything else that happened in the interrogation." I was tired, so I opted to use my phone instead of telepathy. I filled Hope in, and she said she'd call Winter. Kyle and Forster were the California sorority's problem now.

We all went to bed shortly after that. It had been a long and stressful day, and I needed a good night's sleep.

At six in the morning, I woke to someone banging on the front door. I threw on my robe and tiptoed down the stairs even though I was using a cloaking spell. I looked out the window and saw the chief.

I dropped the cloaking spell and opened the door. "Chief? What is it?"

He stepped inside and closed the door. "It's Palmer. He's missing."

"What? He's probably just sound asleep."

I winced at the light as he flicked it on. "No. You don't understand. We were walking out of the station, talking. One minute he was there, and the next he was gone. The only thing left was his briefcase."

I reached out, and he caught my arm before my knees buckled. I took a deep breath and tried to pull myself together. Now wasn't the time to panic. "He's been snatched?"

"That was my first thought. Maybe by the people you missed yesterday."

What could we do? "Go on into the kitchen. I'll wake everyone up." I ran upstairs while telepathically waking up everyone in my family. *Wake up. Get dressed. There's an emergency. Palmer's been snatched and we don't know where he is.*

I threw on the clothes I'd just taken off a few short hours ago and ran down to the kitchen. The chief was making coffee, goddess bless him.

Hope appeared in the kitchen. "Esther told me there was an emergency. What's wrong?"

"Palmer disappeared in front of my eyes about ten minutes ago."

Hope let out a string of words I didn't realize she even knew. "Let me get everyone else here."

Minutes later, the rest of my family and the sorority were all crowded into the kitchen. "Ladies!" Hope yelled above the din of confused questions. "This is our opportunity to find Kyle and Forster."

Winter and Raven knocked on the door and let themselves in. "We lost them," Raven said.

"We know. Palmer has been kidnapped," my mother said.

Thea moved to stand in front of her mother, so we could all see her. "Did he leave anything behind? Maybe I can find him with it."

Could she? I thought she could only see the past.

"I've got his briefcase out in my car. He dropped it when he disappeared," the chief said.

"Okay. I can work with that."

Instantly, the case appeared on the kitchen table. I wasn't sure which witch conjured it from the car, but it didn't matter. Thea put her hand on the case and closed her eyes. "I can see the parking lot, and the two of you walking out. You both look so tired."

Thea readjusted her grip on the case. "He felt arms on him before anything else and knew what was about to happen. Before he dropped the case, he saw two men, Kyle and Forster. He tried to focus on their faces as he dropped the case."

I was amazed he had the presence of mind to do all that when he knew he was being kidnapped. "Can you tell where they took him?"

Thea hugged the case to her chest. After a moment she opened her eyes. "No. I'm sorry, I can't."

I looked to Winter and Raven. "Where would they have gone? Back to California? Or would they stay here?"

"Or would they go to any other state?" the chief asked.

My heart sank at that thought.

"Let's focus on our two states right now," Grandma said.

"They wouldn't go back to us, we drove them out and have alarms set if either of them return," Winter said.

"Is it possible they went back to Chandler House?" Aunt Lily asked.

"Possibly. But a man like Forster probably has more than one safe house we know nothing about," Winter said.

The chief pulled out his phone and started dialing. "I'm putting out an APB on them."

"No, don't. The person who finds either of them could wind up dead. Let us handle it."

He stopped dialing and put his phone away. "I hate not being the one who can fix all the problems."

Aunt Lily patted his arm. "It's okay, Ray, you'll have a lot to do once we find them."

All this talk was getting us nowhere, and I was feeling desperate. "How are we going to find Palmer? We don't know what they're doing to him, or if he's even still . . ." I began to sob.

Grandma put her arm around me. "Hey, no. They're not going to do anything with him until they get what they want. He's too valuable. Once they get in contact with us, we'll make a plan and get him back. I promise."

Delia handed me a tissue. "Do you really think?"

"Absolutely," the chief said. "Let's all try to remain calm. Lily, pour the coffee, would you?"

Aunt Nadia took three coffee cakes from off the counter and put them on the table. "Now I know why I felt compelled to bake so much yesterday."

The room settled down, and everyone helped themselves. After a few minutes, Christina began to yawn. "Look, if nothing's going to happen, I'd like to go home and get back to sleep. Maybe we can pick this up in the afternoon."

Hope shot her an evil glare. "No. While he's not a member of the sorority, we owe him. He put himself in danger for our cause—to help capture the people we didn't take care of soon enough—and we're going to rescue him."

"Maybe if we go back to Chandler House and look for evidence of safe houses?" I suggested.

"Let's give them a little more time to contact us. They didn't take Palmer for no reason," Grandma said.

I pushed my piece of coffee cake around on my plate, but I couldn't eat. Winter gasped, and I looked up to see what was wrong. A half-size image of Forster and Kyle, holding a bloody Palmer between them, stood on the center of the kitchen table.

"Glad to see we have your attention," Forster said.

"Mother, how did they break our wards?" I heard my mother ask Grandma. Grandma just shushed her.

"An excellent question, Michelle. I'm sure you'll figure it out, eventually," Kyle said.

Behind the image, Anna was casting a spell but I couldn't recognize it.

"Let's get down to business. You have my people. I want them back. If you release them within the next fifteen minutes, we'll let Palmer go. If you don't, I'll let the rest of my people use him for practice."

"How can we find you to let you know they're gone?" Hope asked.

"I've got people watching the station. I'll know. Fifteen minutes starts now."

"What in the blue blazes was that?" the chief asked.

"Simple projection. It's a fairly easy spell, though a bit harder to do with a non-magic person," Sasha said.

"Let's focus now. Chief, you need to leave and make it look like you're about to set them free. You could be watched at any time, so make it look good."

He nodded. "I'll call Lily if anything happens."

Once he left, Hope turned to Anna. "Did you find their location?"

"They're here in Portsmouth, outside, near the water."

"Prescott Park?" I asked.

"I think so," Anna said.

"Okay. Spread out around the edges of the park and work your way in. We'll surround them and rescue Palmer," Hope said.

Before I could ask exactly how we were going to rescue him, my mother grabbed my arm and I found myself standing behind a tall rhododendron bush.

The person standing next to me wasn't my mother though. I stepped away and she dropped the glamour from her face. I had to get used to casting more than one spell at a time. I chose a small child glamour and reached up to hold my mother's hand. We started walking toward the center of the park, looking for anything or anyone out of place.

Grandma sent us a telepathic message. I've got two men sitting on either side of a woman, each have their arm around her. Could be them. They're by the fountain.

We moved toward the fountain. I focused on the three people Grandma described, but I didn't feel any magic from them. A strong magician would be able to mask his spells, so that didn't necessarily mean anything. We walked right in front of them as my mother explained the history of the two bridges, almost side by side, that led into Maine.

As we walked by, the woman started to whistle Darth Vader's theme. It was a struggle not to look, but I knew that was Palmer. *It's them. Palmer is the woman.*

My mother bent down to retie my shoelaces as everyone else took their places.

Grandma started giving instructions. I'm behind them. I'll grab Palmer and teleport home. Everyone else, hold Forster and Kyle until Hope and Winter grab them and bring them to the station. Everyone ready? In three . . . two . . . one.

She didn't give anyone time to protest, so we all jumped into action. Palmer vanished, and I felt bad for him, being yanked this way and that with no control. I focused my will on Forster, trying to keep him from using magic. He fought back and slowly was able to raise his hand.

He murmured two words that I didn't hear, and Kyle burst into flames. I'm not going to lie, I took my focus off Forster for an instant. Apparently so did everyone else, because he teleported away. Kyle stood up and staggered to the ground. I ran to him and covered him with my body, trying to put the flames out. My mother grabbed his arm and they disappeared.

CHIVE RIGHT IN

I rolled over in the grass, panting and sweating. I smelled burned clothing and hair and wished for a breeze to take it all away.

My aunts and cousins kneeled beside me. "Don't move, honey," Aunt Nadia said. "I'll heal your burns right away."

I didn't feel like I'd been burned, but I looked down to see large holes burned through my clothes and red blisters forming on my skin. I closed my eyes and waited for someone to tell me what to do. Aunt Nadia was chanting softly, and I felt a cool, soothing mist on my skin.

My mother returned. "Is she okay?"

I opened my eyes. "I'll be fine. You got him to the station?"

"I did. He isn't going anywhere now."

She stroked my hair as the soothing mist returned my skin to its regular shade.

I sat up to see I was surrounded by witches. "Any idea where Forster went?"

No one had any idea.

Aunt Nadia took my mother's hands and healed her burns. I looked to my mother. "Can we go home now? I need to change."

Chapter 20

Although I said I didn't need the help, my mother and Aunt Lily helped me into the house. Palmer panicked when we opened the door and rushed to pick me up. "Where are you hurt? Do you need a doctor?" He rushed me into the living room and set me down on a couch.

"I'm fine. I promise. The aunts already healed my burns."

He looked closely at my clothes. "Broomsticks, Isabella, what happened to you?"

I couldn't help myself. I burst out laughing. "I'm really starting to rub off on you, if you're using witches' expletives." I sat up and ignored the small bout of dizziness. "I'm fine. My clothes took the brunt of the fire."

"There was no fire when your grandmother grabbed me," he said.

"I know. You were surrounded by witches and, once you were safely away, Forster began to feel a little desperate. We were keeping the two of them from teleporting away and closing in on them. Forster set Kyle on fire and, as you can imagine, that disrupted our focus. Forster got away, and I tackled Kyle to put him out."

"And that's how you got burned?"

I nodded. "Honestly, I'm fine. You should ask Aunt Nadia about her burn healing spell. It's amazing."

"Where's Kyle now?"

"The plan was for him to be dropped off at the station. My mother teleported him, ask her."

My mother, who had been listening in the hallway, joined us. "I brought him to the police station, still on fire. It took three fire extinguishers to put him out, so the chief insisted we call an ambulance."

"We've got to get someone there. As soon as he realizes what's going on, he'll escape."

My mother sat next to me. "Hope is there now. She's got him trapped in the room but if the fraternity comes for him, she doesn't think she can fight them off on her own."

I stood up. "Give me two minutes to change and we'll go. I want to question him the second he comes around."

I threw my clothes away, wishing I'd worn one of the self-cleaning outfits Delia had made me. I threw on fresh jeans and a sweater and rushed downstairs to the kitchen. My mother handed me an elastic for my hair. "You're going to need a trim, but this will do for now."

I closed my eyes and sighed. "Fine. I'll do it later." I pulled my hair back and felt burned ends on the left side of my head.

Grandma handed me a wet paper towel. "Get the soot off your face as you're driving, and you'll be fine."

I grabbed my bag. "Ready?"

He nodded and we left. "That's quite a support team you've got there."

I pulled the sun visor down and looked in the mirror. It would probably be best not to look like I needed medical attention while at the hospital. "We do a good job taking care of each other."

"They were as fast and organized as a pit crew. Each person did one thing you'd need. Nadia made you tea, and I think she enchanted it somehow, because she whispered over it before she put it in the travel mug. Delia made you toast, Thea added a banana, and Lily gave me a lecture about bringing you home so you could rest."

I laughed. "Yeah, that's my family."

Palmer looked away and I felt a pang in my heart. Who did he have to look after him? No one. He'd just been kidnapped and he was still going. "Want some toast? I bet she made enough for both of us."

I didn't wait for an answer, but opened the plastic zip of the bag and handed him a slice. He took it and ate it in about three bites. "I take it they didn't feed you?"

"Doesn't matter."

Yes, it did matter, but we'd have time to talk about what happened to him after we questioned Kyle. I flipped the top of the travel mug open. Aunt Nadia had cast a little spell over the tea. "The tea's got a spell of strength and clarity in it. Perfectly safe to drink and, honestly, something I think we both need. Do you want some?"

He looked to me and I could tell he was weighing his options. I was relieved in this pivotal moment he chose to trust me and my family. "Yes. Thanks."

He downed half the tea. "Amazing. I feel like a new man. You drink the other half."

I handed him another slice of toast and ate one myself. Aunt Nadia spread her homemade orange marmalade on it. Delicious. We pulled into the parking lot of the police station, and I handed him the last piece of toast.

He parked and gave me the side-eye. "I shouldn't eat more than you."

"I had coffee cake earlier. You eat this, and you can cook me dinner later this week to make up for it."

He got out of the car. "It's a deal."

I downed the rest of the tea on our way in. Aunt Nadia had cast a potent spell over it, and I felt like I'd just come back from the best vacation ever—ready to take on anything the world could throw at me.

We bypassed the reception desk and went straight to the elevators. Palmer hit the button for the fifth floor.

"You know where Kyle is?"

"Patients in police custody are always in a small ward on the fifth floor. One door with automatic locks."

I had no idea there was such a thing as a secure ward to keep prisoners from posing a threat to other patients. "What's the plan?"

"I want to talk to his doctor, see how long he needs to be here. Then I want Hope to heal him enough that he won't die and then get him back to the security of the station. I don't want to take any more chances with members of the fraternity."

"Aren't your cells already overcrowded?"

"No. The chief and I pulled an all-nighter to get them all moved out. That's why I was so hungry. We were planning to get breakfast when I"—he shuddered—"got taken."

I wondered if there was something I could give him that would keep him safe from teleportation. His birthday was . . . shoot! It was tomorrow.

The elevator doors opened and I followed Palmer to the end of a hallway. Red lights lit the door.

"Red lights mean there's someone in police custody here." He pushed the intercom button.

"Yes?" a crackly voice answered.

"Detective Palmer, Portsmouth PD to see the prisoner."

Hope shimmered into view in front of the door. "All quiet so far," she said, then recast her invisibility spell.

"I'm going to need you in a few minutes. Follow us in," Palmer told her.

I had to admit, he was taking well to magic being performed all around him. The door buzzed and we walked in.

Palmer held his ID out for the nurse and introduced me. "My associate, Miss Proctor."

The nurse nodded. "He's in room one."

"Has he woken up yet?" Palmer asked.

The nurse shook her head. "I told your chief I'd call when he did."

"Can you page his doctor? I need to speak with him."

We walked into room one and looked at the burned, sleeping man.

Cast a little sleeping spell on him to keep him docile, Hope said.

Palmer's eyes widened. "Was that Hope?"

I nodded.

"Cool. Hope, can you heal him most of the way and wake him up? I want the doctor to release him to us."

Can do.

Before our eyes, his burns lessened and he slowly woke up. He saw me and flinched, pulling his arm and the handcuff as far away from me as he could.

"That's right. There's no escape," I said.

He closed his eyes and sighed. "Forster isn't coming for me, is he?"

"Unlikely," Palmer said, "since he was the one who decided to use you like a campfire marshmallow. But today's your lucky day. I'll trade you a pleasant life sentence in jail for a full confession."

"I don't see how life in prison is lucky," he said.

"Once you confess, you'll never be safe on the streets again," I said.

"And if I don't tell you anything? The fraternity has good lawyers, and they'll get me off on a technicality."

Palmer looked around. "Funny, I don't see any lawyers here. You'd think Forster would have sent one to you already." Palmer leaned over the bed. "But maybe he's happy to be rid of you. Maybe he thinks you're already dead."

A man in crisp blue scrubs and a white lab coat walked into the room. "Detective Palmer?"

Palmer turned and shook his hand. "Yes."

"I'm Dr. Nelson."

"I need this man released as soon as possible. I'm no doctor, but he doesn't look too bad to me," Palmer said.

"Let me check his injuries. If you could wait outside, please?"

Palmer and I left the room. I wasn't sure if Hope came with us or not, but I supposed it didn't matter. What Kyle didn't know wouldn't hurt him.

Dr. Nelson joined us in the hallway after a few minutes. "I've never seen such quick healing from burns before. Was he treated at your station before he came here?"

"I don't think so. But you could ask the paramedics who brought him in. Is he fit to travel?"

Dr. Nelson nodded. "I'll do his discharge papers now. The sooner we get him out of here, the better I'll feel."

He went to the nurses' station and started typing on the computer.

"Hope, are you here?" Palmer asked.

Yes.

"Good. We're going to wheel him out of this wing to the elevator. I need you to keep him from vanishing until we're in the elevator. Then you take him directly to the holding cells. Can you do that?"

Isabella, I'll need you to help keep him in the chair. To get him healthy enough to travel, I had to heal him enough that I think he could teleport.

"No problem. And this time I won't lose my focus."

The nurse wheeled Kyle out to us. "We'll take him from here. For safety reasons," Palmer said.

I put my hand on Kyle's shoulder, hoping I'd be able to feel any spells he was preparing to use. The nurse opened the ward doors for us and turned the red lights off. Once we exited the ward, a fire alarm went off. I kept all my focus on Kyle.

Water sprinklers sprayed old, fetid water on us, but I held my focus tight. We began to walk faster toward the elevators.

Palmer hit the button and the doors opened. Thank Brigid for that. We walked in and, before the doors closed, Kyle was gone.

"Hope?" I said, but she didn't answer.

Palmer pressed the button for the fourth floor. "We'll get out here, ditch the wheelchair, and walk down the stairs with everyone else."

He pulled out his phone and dialed the chief. "Are they there?"

Palmer hung up. "She did it."

I let out a deep breath. "Now what?"

"Now I bring you home. I go in and do some paperwork, then take the rest of the day off."

Not even a whole day? That wasn't enough. "You deserve more than that off. But you aren't going to interrogate him?"

"No. The chief and Hope are. He called when you were getting dressed to tell me in no uncertain terms that I need to step away from this case."

"But why?"

"Departmental policy. I can't be impartial toward a man who kidnapped me. And he thinks you can't either."

I thought about that for a minute. "He's right."

"I'm sure the chief will make me take more time and talk to our therapist about the kidnapping."

"How about we go for a run tomorrow morning?" I asked.

"You're serious about getting into better shape?"

I nodded. "If I'm going to be chasing people down with you, yes. It's going to be a long time before I master teleportation, and it's not good to use when people can see you."

"Six o'clock then."

"Let's make it seven."

Chapter 21

Palmer dropped me off at Proctor House, because the cats were still at my apartment. They'd had a hard separation, and I didn't mind letting them stay there until they were ready to come back to the rest of the family. Besides, we had a birthday breakfast to prepare for.

My first stop was to Grandma, who was reading by the living room fireplace. "I need your help."

She put the book down. "You want me to cut your hair?"

Perish the thought. "No, I'm going to let a professional take care of that. I need a present for Palmer's birthday tomorrow."

"What did you have in mind? The way that boy looks at you, you don't need a love spell."

I rolled my eyes. "No. He's held up well with all the magic going on over the past few days, but he's shaken up from being kidnapped. Do we have something, like an amulet, that will keep him protected from magic?"

I'd cast a short-term spell on him once to keep him safe from Wolfe and Stabby, but I wanted something permanent, and something he could see.

"Let me go look in a few texts. I'm not sure I can have something ready for tomorrow. Maybe in a week or two."

She left me alone in the living room. I stared into the fire and let my thoughts wander. When we met, he had been absolutely certain he was putting me in danger, but the reality was my life and my work with the sorority put his life at risk. If we hadn't rescued him—if he didn't have the presence of mind to let me know that was him under the glamour—we could be planning a funeral instead of a birthday party.

I had to take my responsibilities to him seriously. And what if Kate, or Papatonis, or any other officers got caught up in an investigation like Sullivan had? Could we, as a family, do something to keep them all safe? Safe, but ignorant?

Trina might have had the answer for that. I closed my eyes and woke up feeling cold, because the fire had gone out. The sun had set and someone had come in and draped an afghan over me. I levitated more wood to the fire and set it alight with a snap of my fingers.

My stomach growled, so I stood up and walked to the kitchen.

Aunt Nadia was taking eggs out of the refrigerator. "You didn't tell me tomorrow was the detective's birthday. What time are we celebrating, and what would you like me to make?"

I kissed her cheek. "You're amazing. We've got a date to go for a run at seven, so I was thinking a surprise breakfast when we get back. Can you manage that?"

She scoffed. "Of course I can."

The house seemed quieter than usual. "Where is everyone?"

"They're working on the gift. Grandma thinks they can have it done tonight with everyone helping."

I yawned and looked at the clock. It was only eight, but I was ready for bed.

Aunt Nadia opened the refrigerator. "You need dinner before you go to sleep. Sit down and I'll heat you something up."

I did as I was told, and she set a warm plate of meatloaf, mashed potatoes, gravy, and green beans in front of me. Who needed a microwave when you've got magic? My first bite was heavenly. "Delicious. Did you cast a spell over this like you did the tea?"

"No. You don't need it. You're just hungry. I've been laughing over your growling stomach for the last hour."

I finished my dinner and went to bed. My last thoughts were how happy I was to have family to love and protect me.

I woke three minutes before my alarm went off. I reached out in the dark for my phone and checked for text messages, hoping Palmer had canceled our run, or at least pushed it back to noon. No such luck.

I had half an hour to get ready—plenty of time, since this would be the most low-glamor date ever. I wasn't even going to shower first. Once I was dressed and ready, I went downstairs to find Aunt Nadia hiding food in the dining room. "Good morning, sweetie. Just don't let him come in here until after your run, okay?"

A piece of bacon fell from a plate into my hand. I swear it did. I'd never be caught swiping bacon before breakfast was ready. "Is there coffee?"

"As if you have to ask."

We walked into the kitchen, where the rest of my family was waiting, each one of them with dark circles under their eyes.

"It took more time than I hoped, but we did it," Grandma said as she handed me a gold band on a chain.

Tears welled in my eyes as I looked from Grandma, to the aunts, and my cousins. "Thank you. What does it do?"

"It's the mother lode of shield spells, all in one ring. I can't think of any magic that will work on him if he's wearing it," Grandma said.

I looked closely at the ring, seeing the magic pulsing from it. It was easily the strongest single magic artifact I'd ever seen.

"Just needs you to put one more spell on it," Grandma said.

Me? It was already stronger than anything I could conjure up.

"Close your hand around the ring and focus your intention for him to be safe. That's all it needs."

I picked up the ring, closed my eyes and thought about how important Palmer's safety was to me. When I finished, I put it back in its box. Before I closed the box, a thought occurred to me. "But it's a gold band. It's going to look like a wedding ring," I said.

"That's where the chain idea came in. Your mother suggested it. He can wear it under his clothing and no one will be the wiser."

"And once the two of you get married, it can be his wedding ring, so that problem's already been solved for you," Delia said.

"We're a long way from thinking about marriage, but where did the ring come from?" I asked.

"It was your father's," my mother said.

She'd kept his ring in her jewelry box for all these years, hoping he'd return. "Oh no, Mom. You can't . . . I can't take this away from you."

"I want him to have it. Even if things don't work out between the two of you, he's earned it."

I hugged my mother and we both started crying.

"Get a grip on yourselves, you don't want to have red puffy eyes when he gets here, do you? Then you'll have to explain why you were crying, and ruin the surprise of the gift," Grandma said.

I released my mother and wiped my eyes with my sleeve. "I'd like to give it to him before we leave. Is that okay?"

Aunt Lily handed me a tissue. "It's your gift for him, you can give it to him whenever you want."

Thea handed me a jewelry box, and I snapped the lid shut on the ring just as there was a knock on the door. My mother flicked her finger and opened it.

"Good morning," Palmer said and stopped in the doorway. "I wasn't expecting to see you all so early."

Aunt Lily guided him to the table. "How are you? Did you get any sleep last night? Let me pour you a cup of coffee before you go out."

Palmer looked at me and I shrugged.

Aunt Lily set a coffee mug in front of him and said, "Well, I guess we'll all go and give you two some space."

That was my aunt, Captain Obvious.

"What was that all about?" Palmer asked once they were all gone.

I sat next to him and took his hand in mine. "I wanted to give you your birthday gift before we went out."

I handed him the jewelry box and he looked concerned. "I don't know what to say."

"There's a story behind the gift, and it's not what you think, so don't jump to any conclusions," I said.

He didn't look less concerned, but he opened it. "It's a . . . wedding ring?"

I took a deep breath. "No, and yes."

"I'm not sure what to do with that," he said slowly.

"It was a wedding ring, but it isn't now. It's a magical charm that will keep people from using magic on you. My mother thought you'd rather wear it on the chain."

He nodded. "Any magic?"

"All magic. Good or evil intent. So no more teleportation against your will."

He slumped back in his chair and let out a long sigh. "This is amazing." He put it on. "Can we test it out?"

"Sure. Stand up and I'll throw a few spells at you."

He stood and I tried to levitate him. It felt like he wasn't there for me to use magic on.

"Okay, go ahead."

"I am. You're not levitating." I filled the kitchen with fog and could not make it go closer than two feet to him.

"Whoa," he said in a whisper.

"I can't force the fog closer to you," I said as I let it disappear.

"And this will work for any witch? Of any strength?" he asked.

"It carries the strength of all the Proctor witches, so I think so, yes."

He pulled me into his arms. "This is the best gift ever. Thank you so much."

I laughed. "Of course it is. It's a magic ring."

He let me go and sat back down. "That's not what I meant. It's the best gift because it's exactly what I needed. I spent last night terrified something would happen to me."

"You did? Why didn't you call? I could have come over and stayed with you." I wanted to make a joke about being his big strong protector, but it wasn't the right time.

"I can't have you spending your time protecting me. You have your own work to do. At about three this morning, I started devising a really over-the-top gym schedule, so that even if I couldn't beat someone with magic, if I got in the first punch I'd be okay."

I put my hands on his cheeks and kissed his forehead. I was pretty sure Grandma was watching somewhere. "Oh, honey, no. That's not how any of this works. If a witch is concerned about your strength, they'll just strike from a distance."

He took my hands in his and kissed them. "That's why I tore up the pages before I left the house. Your world is terrifying to me, because I don't know enough about it. It's like I'm a kid abandoned in the middle of a war zone. At any minute, something or someone could hurt me, but I don't have enough experience to know what to stay away from."

"We can work on that. And most of your days don't involve magic. You're going to be just fine. But if you didn't get any sleep last night, are you sure you want to go for a run this morning? We could skip it and go straight to your birthday breakfast."

His eyes gleamed. "Birthday breakfast? Is that a thing in your family?"

As if on cue, the rest of the family came rushing in, wearing party hats and blowing whistles. I knew Grandma had been listening to us!

"Breakfast is waiting for you in the dining room," Aunt Nadia said.

She must have been cooking most of the night. There was more food on the table than we'd eat in a week of breakfasts.

"Before we begin, I'd like to take a minute to say something," Palmer said.

We all looked at him, and I probably wasn't the only one who hoped he'd be quick so we could get to the mountain of pancakes, and sausage, and bacon, and eggs, and waffles, and muffins, and fruit on the table.

"I know when we first met, I didn't trust this family, and I doubt you all trusted me. I have had a radical change of attitude toward the Proctor family, and I can't believe how kind and generous you have all been to me." He took hold of his ring. "This gift shows me how much you value me. And Michelle, the fact that you'd give up your husband's ring for my protection"—he paused and blinked back tears—"gives me a standard to live up to."

He picked up his glass of orange juice. "I know it's a little early in the morning for toasts, but I'd like to toast your family, and the way you all selflessly step up when you're needed."

He raised his glass and took a sip. We did likewise. It looked like my mother was about to say something, but Grandma cut her off.

"If you need to, you can give a speech later on, Michelle, but for now, let's eat."

The End

Why is Inanna so cruel to her witches? Find out in the Chive Right In bonus scene.

LisaBouchard.com/CRIBonus

Excerpt from About Thyme

Chapter 1

I picked up my coffee mug and took a long sip. When I set the opening time of my business to ten in the morning, I wanted to sleep in, not to race to seven o'clock breakfast dates with my boyfriend. And yet, here I sat across from him at The Crispy Biscuit. The February sun wasn't even up high enough to warm the air and today felt like a day for a never-ending mug of something warm.

February always brought out the winter doldrums in me. Not enough sun, not enough fresh air, not enough of anything that made me happy. I'd taken to spending more time in my heated greenhouse to breathe in the deep, earthy smell of living plants and even that hadn't helped much.

Palmer waved his hand in front of my face. "Hey, are you listening?"

I frowned. "Sorry, I drifted off for a minute. I told you I wasn't great first thing in the morning. What were you saying?"

"Drink more coffee, it'll help."

I took another sip as he repeated his question to me.

"What do you want to do for Valentine's Day? And do you even celebrate it?"

"What do I want to do? How about a cruise in the Bahamas? I need some bright, warm sunlight. And no, we don't celebrate it, but it's not off limits. Saint Patrick's day is right out, though."

Emma stopped at our table with breakfast. I'd ordered orange buttermilk pancakes with citrus syrup in an attempt to capture a tropical feeling in my day. "Here you go," Emma said. "Let me know if you need anything else. And Isabella, I'd love to catch up today. Do you have any free time?"

Emma and I had been friends since high school and in all that time she'd never asked to catch up, she usually just launched into whatever she wanted to say. "I'll be at the apothecary all day, why don't you stop in when your shift is over?"

She smiled. "You bet. I get out at eight."

"I wonder what that was about," I said.

Palmer took a bite of sausage and shrugged. "I can't get the time off for a cruise, but let me look into something a little more local."

I hadn't expected we'd go on a cruise. We weren't at the shared vacation stage in our relationship. "That was just wishful thinking. Something closer to home would be great. You haven't failed me yet."

We continued to eat, but I could tell there was something he wanted to ask me. "Out with it."

He looked uncomfortable. "It's not a question for here. I'll ask when we're done."

That was interesting. Was it a personal question, or was it a sorority or witch question? Was it something entirely different that I couldn't imagine? I started to eat my pancakes. The sooner I finished, the sooner I'd find out.

"Have you got any interesting cases going on?" I asked.

"Nah. Seems like no one wants to go through the effort in the cold. Kate and I are working on some shoplifting cases, but that's it. How's business at the apothecary?"

"It's good. Tea sales are through the roof and it's hard to keep anything with cinnamon in stock. Mackenzie and I are spending today bagging loose leaf tea so people can buy it right off the shelf."

He put his fork down, his breakfast eaten. "Cinnamon?"

"It's great for winter. If you've got just a little bit of cinnamon, you get that feeling of warm baked goods. If it's a stronger flavor, it's spicier and you can feel heat on your tongue. I'll make you some and you can see."

My pancakes were gone and the citrus had made me feel a little sunnier on the inside. I was counting on spicy cinnamon tea to do the rest for me today.

Palmer dropped money on top of our bill. It was a very rare date that I got to pay for. When we first met, I was basically broke, working two jobs to make sure I could pay bills every month. With each passing month, I was getting closer to what the internet told me was an average detective salary. In another year I might make more than him.

I waved to Emma as we walked out. "I'll see you later on."

I wrapped my arm around his and looked to see if we were alone on the sidewalk. "Now that we're out here, what did you want to ask me?"

He pulled his scarf up. "If you want to go somewhere warm and sunny, why not just teleport yourself there?"

I laughed. "I thought you had some sort of serious question that I should be worried about. It's hard work to teleport and the further you go, the more problems you have. I can't teleport myself anywhere yet and it would be exhausting for Jameson to bring me that far."

He steered me around a slushy puddle. "But what about people going to and from California?"

"I can't imagine how difficult it was for them. I suppose if I needed to go somewhere, my mother could take me, or Grandma, but can you imagine me asking Grandma to take me on a vacation?"

He frowned. "But she'd be on vacation too."

He had a good point. "Maybe it's just not a thing my family does. I'll have to ask."

I opened the apothecary door. "Are you ready for some fantastic tea?"

He stomped the snow off his shoes and followed me in. "Absolutely, I'd like the spicier one, please."

I started my morning routine of putting my things away, lighting Trina's candle, and saying a few words to her. Today I was self-conscious talking to a lit candle but I did it anyway. "Hope it's warm and sunny where you are, Trina. I don't think we've seen the sun for two weeks at this point and I'm in serious need of sunlight."

Palmer waited respectfully until I was done speaking. "Do you talk to her every day?"

I turned to him. "Yes. I started because I missed her so much and had no idea how to run this business. I was scared and talking to the candle and her photo helped me imagine what she'd say to me."

He looked around the apothecary with the new displays I'd installed to hold the expanded inventory. "Looks like it worked. I think she'd be proud of you. I'm proud of you. You've done amazing things here, and have made a place for yourself in the sorority, help me solve more cases than I'm comfortable admitting to, and you're still just you."

I smiled. I come from an old New England family and random compliments aren't a part of every day life for us. "What do you mean I'm just me though?"

"You're still kind, still thoughtful, still fun and funny and even though you've seen a lot of death it doesn't seem to have affected you too badly. Unless you're not telling me."

He was right. The death I'd seen hadn't fundamentally altered my outlook on life. "Does that make me weird? Shouldn't I be more affected than I am? Because I'm not holding out on you - no nightmares I don't tell you about, and I'm really only worried when we haven't caught someone yet."

"Have you ever considered joining the police, officially? You've got the right mindset for it and I bet having the chief and me as a reference would get you in."

I shook my head. "No way. I'll stick with the sorority." I started to make hot cinnamon tea for the day. "Not that I don't like working with you on cases, but I like having a few things to focus on. Maybe that's why I'm okay with all the violence. I also have to spend a lot of my time thinking about new tea blends, or what I need to order for the shop, or how the cats are doing, or any of the other hundred things I have to keep track of in my day. I don't have time to obsess over murders once they're solved."

I handed him a mug. "I like it best plain, but if you don't there's cream and sugar on the table."

He sipped and his eyes flew open. Once he swallowed, he started to cough. "Spicy!"

"I warned you," I said, taking his mug back so he wouldn't spill the tea.

"I see what you mean about it keeping me warm. This would be perfect for a cold winter stake out."

I handed him his mug. "I bet it would. How many stake outs do you do?"

"Not many. I leave them to Papatonis."

I reached up to take a box of the tea off the shelf. "Here. Give this to him with my thanks."

He took the tea and pulled me into his arms. "This is exactly what I mean."

I turned my face up to his. We weren't a kiss in public kind of couple, but we've had our moments. His lips brushed mine and the door chimes rang.

Chapter 2

"Oh, sorry," I heard Emma say. "I'll wait outside."

We quickly separated. "Don't be silly. Come on in."

Palmer picked up the tea. "I'll bring this to Papatonis this morning. I'm sure he'll appreciate it."

Once Palmer left, Emma squealed. "You were kissing!"

I poured myself a mug of tea. "Want some? It's spicy."

"I'll take some, but tell me about the kissing."

I handed her the mug and poured another one. "It was just one little kiss. We've been dating for a while now and I think it's about time."

She followed me as I walked to the back of the apothecary. "You can put your coat in the office, then we're going to work in the prep room."

"You two always look so...platonic whenever I see you. It's hard to tell you're a couple at all."

I pulled down four boxes of tea ingredients and set them on the counter. Emma must not have been paying close attention because Palmer had a look that he reserved for me. A look that said I was all he was paying attention to in the entire universe. "Just because we aren't all over each other in public doesn't mean we're not a couple."

"I know, it's just, I want you to be happy." She sat on one of the stools. "And speaking of happy, I've got something I want to talk to you about."

Her grin was off the charts huge. "Let me guess, a boyfriend who kisses you in public all the time."

She opened the box of lavender in front of her. "Better than that."

I turned to her and laughed. "Two boyfriends who kiss you in public all the time? That seems like it could be a problem if they don't know about each other."

She pulled the lavender out of the box. "Would you get serious for a minute? I've changed my religion."

I didn't see that coming. Emma wasn't a particularly religious person. She had a Christmas tree every December and an Easter basket in the spring, but that was about the extent of it. "What was your religion before? I don't think I even know."

"Episcopal? Presbyterian? One of those where I never even understood what the title meant. But she was some denomination of Christian.

"Okay, so what are you now?" I asked.

"I want to see if you can guess. My new religion is more free-form, where you find the things you believe within you instead of being told what you should believe."

That was an easy one. "Unitarian Universalist. That was easy."

"No, but I can see why you'd think that. My new religion is much more egalitarian, there's no guy up at the front of a church telling us we're all sinners."

I used a scoop to measure out cinnamon from the box in front of me. "Are you a Reform Jew?"

She shook her head. "No. This religion is much more earth-centric, no monotheistic tendencies."

I thought for a minute. This was getting tougher. "Uh, are you Hindu?"

Emma laughed "No. I'm just going to tell you. I'm a wiccan."

I almost dropped the scoop of cinnamon I was measuring out. "You're what now?"

"I'm a wiccan and I belong to a fantastic new coven."

This was bad. Very, very bad. The coven system had been abandoned in favor of family-based groups because the power dynamics were too complicated otherwise. Emma didn't know that. A knot formed in the pit of my stomach that someone was trying to take advantage of her. But then I realized that couldn't be the case—Emma wasn't a witch. "Do I call you a wiccan, or a witch, or what?"

"We prefer the term wiccan," she said solemnly. "Witch has such ugly connotations, don't you think?"

I didn't, but I wasn't going to tell her that. I pushed the boxes out of my way and sat on the stool next to hers. "Can I ask you questions? I don't know anything about this so don't hate me if I sound stupid, okay?"

She beamed at me. "Of course not. Anger is not our way. Ask me anything you want."

Anger is not our way? Someone should let Grandma know that. "How did you find this coven?"

"I haven't been happy lately, and I wonder if being a waitress was all my life had to offer. Was there more to life, or could I make my life more meaningful?"

I nodded. If I hadn't inherited the apothecary I'd have the same thoughts she was.

"One morning a guy left me a flyer along with my tip. It was an invitation to visit the coven and see if it was right for me. I figured why not? The meeting was in a hotel conference room, how dodgy could it be?"

An excellent question. I don't think she'd like my answer, though. "Okay, so you went to the meeting. What happened that made you think it was for you?"

"Did you ever meet a person and just know you were going to be friends? You just clicked and that was it? That's how I felt about Winslow. And it's odd because he's old, at least fifty, and not the kind of guy I'd ordinarily pay attention to unless he was a customer."

"Could he do magic? Like, did he have real powers that he showed you?"

She took another sip of her tea. "Our coven is devoted to more mental talents. He read my mind and told me about how I was seeking a fresh start in life, and how I felt my parents didn't always understand me."

It took all my energy not to roll my eyes at her. Whoever this Winslow was, he was just a garden variety scam artist. "Did he ask you for money?"

She frowned at me. "Of course not. The coven isn't like a regular church that needs so much money for buildings and payroll and flowers and everything else. We're an earth religion and Mother Earth provides for us."

Now I was confused. "How did Mother Earth provide a conference room?"

"I honestly don't know. It didn't occur to me to ask. There were ten of us in the meeting, and four of us decided to join."

"Can you show me your magic powers? Like, can you do stuff that most people can't?"

"Not yet. But I practice every day and I think I'm getting better. My first task is to choose a goal, meditate on it every day and create my own spell to get what I want."

That seemed like the standard advice from every mindset guru, right down to the positive affirmation being relabeled as a spell. "What's your goal?"

"My goal is to remove all the plastic from the oceans."

Certainly a worthy goal, but probably not something she could do with the power of thought alone. "That's a good one. How are you going to do it?"

Her eyes went wide. "I can't tell you my spell. We're supposed to keep those a secret."

I nodded seriously. "I understand. Do you think this will happen soon?"

"No. There are steps we have to go through to before we can expect any of our spells to start working. I'm on the first one." She took a deep breath "Which brings me to why I'm telling you all this. Part of my growth and learning in the coven is to talk to others and bring them to a meeting. Each one of us needs to bring in two other people, so that we've got the magic number of thirteen in the coven. Winslow says that's when we'll see our power start to show."

"Oh, Emma, I don't know about that."

"But think about it, you're an herbalist. You should feel right at home with the whole Mother Earth vibe the coven has."

She wasn't wrong there, but I didn't want to tell her Mother Earth and I had already met. On the other hand, maybe Palmer could do something about him. I was getting a strong MLM vibe from her "coven" and I was afraid Emma would be in too deep by the time he started asking for money. "You know what? Why not? I can't guarantee that I'll join but I can at least go and listen to him."

Emma jumped off her stool and gave me a hug. "Thank you! I just know you're going to love him. The next meeting is Friday at seven, at the Marriott. I'll be there too, so you won't have to worry about being alone."

"Before I go, can I do any research on your coven? I'd love to see what I'm getting myself into."

"I've got a flyer for you to read, hang on." She grabbed her bag from my office and pulled out a printed page.

The first line read Join the coven. "Wait a minute, your coven doesn't even have a name?"

"Not yet. We won't choose one until we have all thirteen members."

I kept reading, but there was nothing useful until I got to the end, where the meeting time and date were listed. "I'll be there."

She gave me another hug. "Thank you. Do you think your cousins would be interested in going? I could go chat with them about it, too."

I thought about that for a minute. I didn't want to drag them to some ridiculous coven information session, but it would be good if I went with some backup. "They might. They don't open until ten, so go ask them later on today." And that would give me time to call them and let them know they needed to say yes to her.

"You're the best. I'm going to let you get back to your work and I'll at least see you on Friday."

Books by Lisa Bouchard

Root Cause
Leaf of Faith
What in Carnation
Romaine Calm
No Big Dill
On a Larkspur
Simply Irisistible
About Thyme

Books by Elle Bouchard

Midlife, Murder, and Magic

About the Author

It all started when she learned to read at five. One of her first and favorite memories is of words taped to all the objects in the house. Not long after that, books became the best thing ever and there was no turning back.

She suffered a crisis of confidence in high school and college and decided writing was too difficult, so she earned a degree in chemistry and later enrolled in a physics PhD program instead. Three career changes and four children later, she's back to writing and much happier for it.

Now she works from her home office in New Hampshire amid the books, kids, and occasional pets.

Visit her at http://LisaBouchard.com.

And http://ElleBouchard.com